FUTURE FRIEND

DAVID BADDIEL

Illustrated by Steven Lenton

HarperCollins *Children's Books*

First published in Great Britain by
HarperCollins *Children's Books* in 2020
Published in this edition in 2021
HarperCollins *Children's Books* is a division of HarperCollins*Publishers* Ltd,
1 London Bridge Street
London SE1 9GF

www.harpercollins.co.uk

HarperCollins*Publishers*
1st Floor, Watermarque Building, Ringsend Road
Dublin 4, Ireland

3

ISBN 978-0-00-833422-2

David Baddiel and Steven Lenton assert the moral right
to be identified as the author and illustrator of the work.

A CIP catalogue record for this title is available from the British Library.

Typeset in ITC Novarese 12/22pt
Printed and bound in England by CPI Group (UK) Ltd, Croydon CR0 4YY

FUTURE FRIEND

Books by David Baddiel

ANIMALCOLM

BIRTHDAY BOY

FUTURE FRIEND

HEAD KID

THE PARENT AGENCY

THE PERSON CONTROLLER

THE TAYLOR TURBOCHASER

To the other member of my family, Stasia K

Hello readers,

Thank you for buying this book (or, at least, for picking it up in the bookshop and reading this bit). I just wanted to let you know something, which is: this story mainly takes place in 2019. Originally, when I started writing it, in January 2020, it mainly took place in 2020. But then things happened in the world – the real world, I mean – which made me think: *Hmm. Might be better to set this story just before all that.*

Actually, some parts of this book take place in 3020. And, as you'll see, the way I wrote the world as it might be in *3020* is kind of a bit like things actually got in *2020* for a while (and I suppose, although hopefully not, might get again). It was almost like I knew what was going to happen. I'd like to go 'weeoooweeoooweeoooweeooo' now (that's the actual word for the music they have in films when a magic thing happens, of course) as if I did magically know that, but I didn't.

Anyway. *Now* this book mainly takes place in 2019, before everything that happened in 2020 happened . . . but what the world is like in 3020 is what the world *might* be like unless we . . . Well, maybe you need to start the book and see.

Enjoy,

David

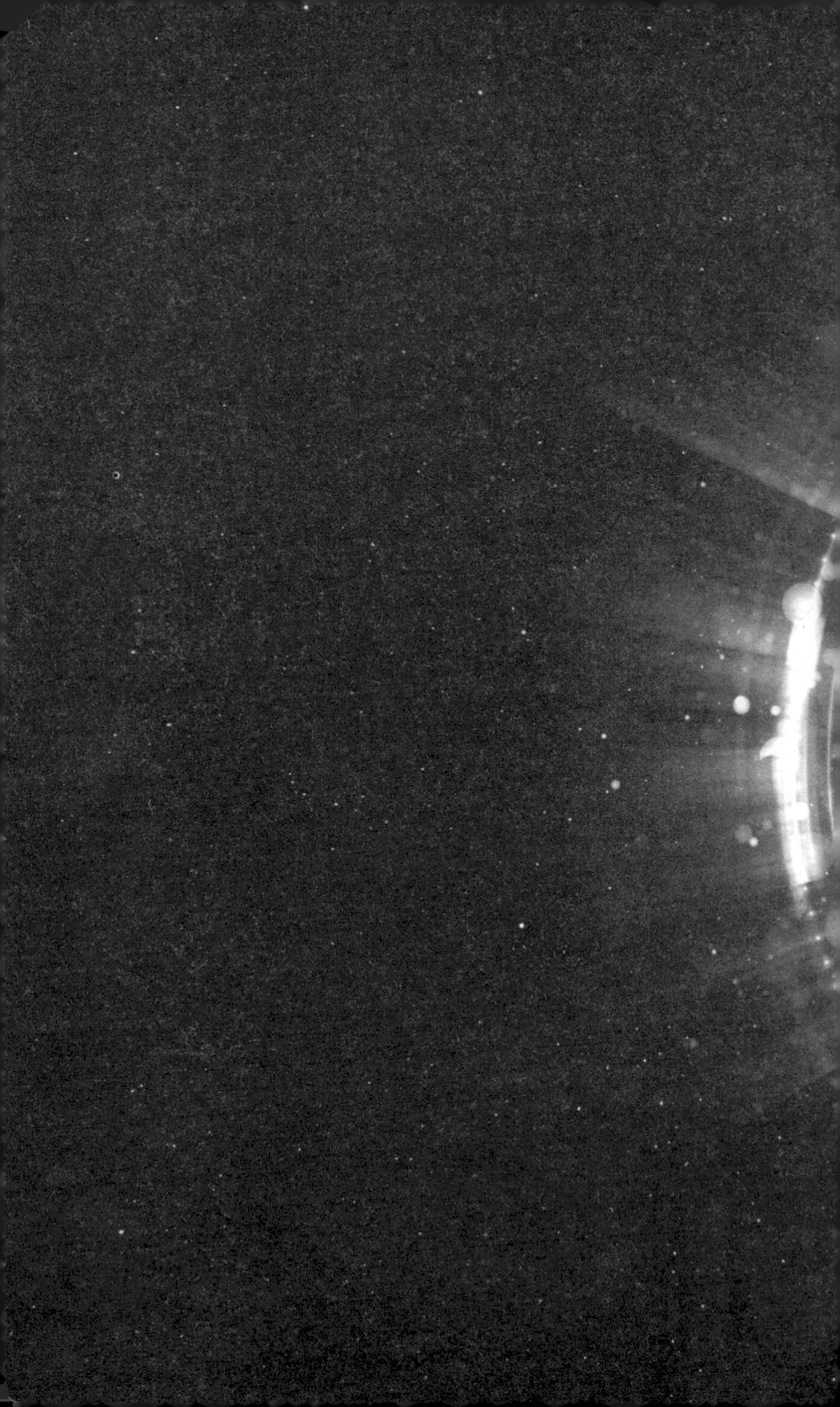

PART ONE

3020

STAY
INSIDE

FLOOD WARNING!
TEMP: 51°C.

CHAPTER 1

The Stadium Above the Clouds

As ever, it was hard for Pip@256X#YY.3_7's mum to get her out of bed. This was because Pip@256X#YY.3_7 was eleven and eleven-year-olds often *are* hard to get out of bed. But it was also because Pip@256X#YY.3_7 slept in a pod that had a built-in DreamSet, and last night she had programmed it for a *Scoring the Winning Goal in the World League Final* dream.

At the point at which her mum started knocking

on the window of her BedPod, Pip@256X#YY.3_7 had, in fact, scored that goal, and celebrated by whooshing round the ground in her GravityLess Boots. But there was still the Great Slide down from the Stadium Above the Clouds to do, and

she wasn't going to miss that: it always looked like such fun when the winning team zoomed down the giant slide, holding up the trophy. So she just let the DreamSet reframe her mum's *Knock! Knock! Knock!* so that it became the crowd chanting, '*Pip! Pip! Pip!*'

The Great Slide down from the Stadium Above the Clouds *was* great. The tallest in the solar system, the slide was made from Graphite42, a metal that was completely friction-free, and Pip whooshed down it at what felt like over a thousand kilostrands a minute! And the view, as she approached the City from above, was fantastic! She was nearly at the bottom when . . .

BUMP!

Her progress was halted by the GravityLess Boots of someone hovering in the way.

'HEY!' shouted Pip, rubbing her face. 'You can't be here!'

'I can,' said the person hovering in the way. 'I'm your mum.'

'I know!' said Pip. 'But this is *my* dream!

'Yes,' said Nina@256X#YY.3_7, 'but I'*m* your mum!'

'You just said that!'

'Yes, but you seem to be forgetting it. And also that I have one of these!'

Nina took from the pocket of her ImageSuit a small crystal inscribed with the words: **DreamSet: Override Control**.

'Oh no . . .' said Pip. 'Mum . . .'

Nina rotated the crystal. Instantly, everything – the Great Slide, the view up to the Stadium Above the Clouds, the view down to the City – dissolved like tears in rain. And was replaced by Pip in her BedPod, looking up at her mum standing outside the window of her pod. Nina's ImageSuit was now set to *StandardMum*. She had her arms crossed.

'*Now* what's going on?' said Pip. 'I thought your Dream Override could only change my dream – not actually wake me up?'

'You're not awake,' said her mum. 'I just changed your dream to this.'

'What . . . I'm now *dreaming* that I'm at home in my pod?'

'Yes.'

'What a rubbish dream!'

'Yes. Which is why you might as well wake up.'

Pip sighed. She blinked three times, and woke up. She stretched, yawned, and pressed the button by the side of her AirMattress. The window of her pod opened with a smooth hiss. She frowned.

'Actually,' she said, '*have* I woken up? Because this looks exactly the same as my dream.'

'Yes,' said her mum. 'Good morning – time for school!'

CHAPTER 2

HouseUnit 72

Luckily for Pip, who felt quite tired after all the dream confusion, school in 3020 was not somewhere you *went*. She did still have to get dressed, and eat breakfast, but it helped that these things didn't involve a lot of effort.

Pip, like everyone in 3020, had a small wireless chip implanted in her brain called a MindLink. The MindLink synced up to some of the items in her HouseUnit. So, when she wanted to get dressed, all she had to do was picture herself wearing her ImageSuit, and immediately it flew out of the cupboard and – once she stuck her arms out – fitted itself round her.

The same with her boots: she lay down on the floor, stuck her legs up, wiggled her feet, then thought about them with boots on, and they – the boots – hovered from the side of the pod (where she'd left them yesterday) and slid themselves on to those very same feet.

Pip's breakfast didn't take much in the way of effort either. Not because the pots and pans and food flew on to the CookStation when she went into the FoodSpace and thought about them via MindLink – although she *could* have done that – but because it was made by someone else. Not her mum or dad: they were already busy working in the LabSpace. No, Pip's breakfast was made by Pip 2.

You'll meet it – no, let's be nice and call it *her* – in a minute.

This morning's breakfast was Pip's favourite: boiled egg and soldiers. (Not a boiled-egg-and-soldiers pill, but real boiled egg and soldiers; just because this is the future doesn't mean everything's going to be like you expect it to be from films. Although obviously the egg *had* been made from chicken cells, not laid by an actual chicken. Actual chickens lived in Zone X, where they had formed a very anti-human army, and refused to lay eggs any more.)

Once Pip had dressed and eaten breakfast, it was indeed time for school. Or, as you would call it if you lived in 3020, the Learning Matrix. TLM was, as you might have guessed, an online school.

I know you might think that *you* do a lot of things online. But, in 3020, *everything* happens online. This is partly because in the future computers are more advanced, but also because almost no one goes outside in 3020. It's too hot or, in some places, too flooded, and also there are some very nasty bugs floating about, some of which come from the mutant animals that have taken over a lot of the Earth, and some of which were produced by humans as weapons, in the various wars between now and then.

This is why Pip's family name was @256X#YY.3_7. With nearly all communication outside the HouseUnit happening by computer, normal surnames had been replaced, a long time before, with an online address. Obviously, with twenty-four billion people in the world – and a whole section of the animal kingdom, particularly the chimps, now online as well – this meant that everyone had to have a long, complicated address.

To start today's lesson, Pip sat in her HouseUnit's MainSpace, and reached for her G-Glasses. Before she put them on though, she looked over to Block 5. Pip and her family – which was just her and her mum and dad, as the Population Police only allowed one child per family – lived in HouseUnit 72. This was about halfway up Block 4, one of twenty enormous skyscrapers in Zone J, one of the poorer zones of the City.

Pip saw that the sky was very red, like it was most of the time, and she could hear – as you could most of the time – the distant sound of thunder. But, across the way, Pip could see the boy in the window of his HouseUnit. He was just about to put on his G-Glasses as well. As he sometimes did, the boy looked up – they both knew what time they were meant to start school – smiled and waved. Pip smiled and waved back. He turned away and put his G-Glasses on.

Pip frowned. She wished she knew him better, but though she could see him clearly – and liked his nice

face and friendly smile – he was too far away for her to ImageSearch for his name.

Pip sighed and put on her G-Glasses. At first, these just looked like ordinary glasses, but, after a second, the lenses went dark. They bleeped, and a series of lights went on around the edges of the lenses. In Pip's vision, a schoolroom appeared, although she was the only pupil.

Miss Lucy was waiting for her.

'Hello, Pip,' she said.

'Hello, Miss Lucy,' said Pip.

'I'll be your teacher today.'

'You're my teacher every day,' said Pip.

Miss Lucy frowned, and the edges of her body froze for a second, then unfroze.

'I have processed that statement, and found it to be a little bit rude,' she said. 'Part of your learning is politeness.'

'Sorry, Miss Lucy.'

'Just because I don't exist is no reason to make fun of me.'

'You do exist,' said Pip.

'Not in the real world,' said Miss Lucy, looking a bit sad. Her body froze and unfroze again. 'Sorry, that was a *Human Emotion* glitch. Anyway,' she said, 'today we're going to be doing history.'

'Oh good,' said Pip. 'Which period?'

'Your favourite. The twenty-first century.'

'Hey,' said a voice to Pip's left, 'no one's fed me my Kitty Chunks.'

CHAPTER 3

A kind of toy

'Hold on, Miss L,' said Pip.

'Is that Squeezy-Paws@256X#YY.3_7?' she replied.

'Yes,' said Pip, taking the G-Glasses off and looking down at a large – really, an absolute unit, a total chonk of a – cat. 'Are you telling the truth?'

'How dare you!' said the cat in a slow, rather posh drawl. 'I *always* tell the truth.'

'No, she doesn't,' said a high-pitched – a better

word would be squawky – voice.

Pip looked over at the BirdCube. Dag – the family's green parrot, who lived in a see-through cube, which hovered below the middle of the ceiling – was staring in a bored way at Squeezy-Paws.

'Shut up, parrot.'

'You shut up, cat.'

'No, you shut up. Fat idiot.'

'Oh, I know you are. But what am I?'

'Guys,' said Pip, 'stop arguing. What's the point of animals evolving speech if that's all you're going to do?'

'I've told you before, Pip,' said Dag, 'saying that

is offensive to parrots. We could speak *centuries* ago! And then, after years of lagging behind, the other animals caught up. But now people forget how we parrots led the way!'

'Well, the truth is, Dag,' said Miss Lucy, appearing as a full-size hologram in the middle of the room, 'that all that parrots *used* to say, in the olden days, was *Pretty Polly! Pretty Polly!* over and over again.'

'That's all you *thought* we were saying,' muttered Dag darkly.

'This is all fascinating,' said Squeezy-Paws, 'but meanwhile who's going to feed me?'

'Not me,' said Dag. 'I can't leave this cube, can I? It's a prison, I tell you, for a bird. I should be allowed to fly! That's what birds do!'

'Dag,' said Pip with

a sigh, 'you know it wouldn't be safe. The air filters would suck you in and you'd be—'

'Yes, yes, I know,' said Dag.

'Um, still hungry here,' said Squeezy-Paws.

'I'll do it!' said Pip 2. 'I'll feed you!'

'Oh, okay, thanks, 2.'

'No problem,' said Pip 2, scooping up the enormous cat and taking her out of the room.

'Ouch! Be careful with those RoboClone hands. They're pokey!' said Squeezy-Paws.

'Sorry!' said Pip 2 as they left the MainSpace.

'The cat's right – someone needs to download some new software for that thing,' said Dag after they'd gone. 'It spilled my seed tray yesterday.'

'*Shh*,' said Pip, 'she'll hear you.'

The parrot stared at her. 'You know it's a robot, right? It's not a real person.'

'It's a clone,' said Pip defensively. 'Of me.'

'It *looks* and *sounds* like you, yes. They've done a great job on the outer skin shell. But inside it's all moving parts. And some of them are rusty.' Dag ruffled his feathers. 'I heard your mum and dad talking about . . . a proper upgrade yesterday. A real upgrade.'

Pip looked round sharply towards the FoodSpace. Pip 2 was feeding Squeezy-Paws, but she was also looking through at them. *Had she heard*? Pip moved closer to Dag, out of the RoboClone's view.

'Getting a new Pip 2, you mean?'

'Yep. Pip 3!' said Dag.

Pip didn't know how to feel about this. Three years ago, her parents had bought her Pip 2 to keep her company. The RoboClone came with a growth cell installed, which meant that as Pip grew so did Pip 2, continuing to look and sound the same as her.

Which sounds like Pip 2 was a kind of toy, but really it was much more than that: Pip 2 used to be Pip's closest friend. They'd done everything together. They'd read together, and fed the pets together, and played all the games together they could within the HouseUnit. They'd even slept in the same bed together – the last thing Pip would say at night was, 'Goodnight, Pip 2!,' and Pip 2 would say, 'Goodnight, Pip!'

But now that Pip was bigger (as, because of the growth cell, was Pip 2), there wasn't room for the RoboClone inside her BedPod. And, as time had gone by, and Pip's parents began working all day in the LabSpace, Pip 2 had ended up spending less time with Pip and more time helping out round the house, cooking and cleaning and fixing things. Which was what Pip's parents needed Pip 2 to do.

So Pip and Pip 2's relationship had changed. It was still a *bit* like having a friend, but, to be honest, Pip thought – and she didn't like thinking it, but she knew it was true – it was a bit *more* like having a twin who was more of a HouseUnitKeeper than a sister.

Plus, Pip's mum and dad didn't have much in

their CryptoCoin account any more, and so some of the updates and fixes needed to keep Pip 2 from glitching had recently not been done.

'Ahem,' said Miss Lucy. 'Any chance of starting this lesson? I mean, I know I'm only a hologram, which means – yes – I don't have a home to go to or anything, but still I think we should get cracking.'

CHAPTER 4
Any questions?

'Sorry,' said Pip, putting her G-Glasses back on.

'Thank you,' said Miss Lucy, disappearing from the real room, and reappearing in the virtual schoolroom. 'So. The twenty-first century . . .'

She lifted her hand, and a HoverScreen appeared. It started playing a film, with images of people walking about on old streets and squares. A deep, reassuring voice said:

'At the start of the twenty-first century, life for

humans was still mainly driven by what used to be called face-to-face contact.'

The screen cut to show some men and women in a café, talking and laughing. Then an image of some other men and women, dressed more smartly, in an office, talking seriously.

'Yes, back then people actually thought that the best way to get things done was to meet, in person, and talk. But it was at this point that . . .'

The film changed to show a man in a room typing on what Pip knew, from other films she'd seen, to be a computer, even though computers in 3020 didn't look anything like that any more. They didn't have keyboards and screens in 3020. If, for example, Pip wanted to search for something on the Grid (what you know as the internet, although a hundred thousand times faster), she would just do it through her G-Glasses, or even directly from her MindLink.

The screen split into two, showing a woman on

a computer. Then it split into four, with a teenager and a child tapping on keyboards. And it carried on splitting and splitting until there were hundreds of people in rooms, all typing on those old computers.

'. . . everyone realised it was much better and quicker to communicate using screens. And, even though it was a very long time ago, this can be said to be the start of our own modern times.'

Miss Lucy raised her hand and the film stopped playing.

'Any questions?'

Yes, thought Pip. *Why does everyone look so lonely*?

But she just shook her head, and Miss Lucy let the film carry on.

CHAPTER 5

Basic regulation

Pip's mum and dad were scientists. They had once worked for the City Government, trying to create inventions to help with the heat and the flooding and the viruses.

But, in the last few years, the City Government had given up on that. Now they spent the bulk of their money just redesigning buildings so that people could live their entire life indoors. The buildings had become taller and taller, and everything the people who lived in them needed was delivered by drones, which buzzed constantly round the high windows, dropping their packages off into chutes that tunnelled straight into every HouseUnit.

But Pip's mum and dad hadn't given up on inventing. They just did their work by themselves (which was why they were running out of CryptoCoin), researching and experimenting at home. Both of them still thought there was a way to make the outside world better. Even though there wasn't much sign of that when you looked out of the window.

On the day Pip was having her history lesson, Pip's mum and her dad – Ivan@256X#YY.3_7 – were in the LabSpace. It was actually just the SpareSpace in their HouseUnit, but since no one ever came to stay her parents had put all their science equipment in there. Sometimes the space went very dark, and then, through the small round window in the LabSpace door, you could see lots of lights twinkling on and off.

Recently, Pip had noticed – and noticed again as she came into the MainSpace, having finished her lesson – that her parents would go in there and not come out for hours. Which was why Pip 2 had been doing so much of the housework.

'Oh my days, what even is this?' asked Squeezy-Paws.

'It's KitABeef Product 67.'

Pip, in the MainSpace, looked over to the FoodSpace. Squeezy-Paws was sitting by her bowl, staring up at Pip 2.

'KitABeef Product 67 tastes like kitty litter. That I've weed and pooed on. I like Kitty Chunks!'

'Oh dear,' said Pip 2, blinking. 'I'm afraid I have run a search through every available cat food and KitABeef Product 67 is the foodstuff recommended for a cat of your size.'

'It isn't even made of real cows,' said Squeezy-Paws,

sniffing her bowl unhappily.

'Of course not!' shouted Dag from his cube. 'A cow is Chancellor of the Exchequer now. And a very good one she is too, in my opinion.'

'Yes, okay,' said Squeezy-Paws. 'But meanwhile you *know* I hate it.'

Pip 2 shook her head at the cat. 'I do not know that. You have never told me.'

'Meow,' said Squeezy-Paws, which she sometimes still said, although always in a deadpan way, like someone saying something they don't really mean. 'I must have told the *real* one then.'

At this, Pip 2 made a face. It seemed, to Pip, looking through from the other room, like an *angry* face. This confused and concerned her. She knew that one of the most basic rules, written into Pip 2's core software, was that a RoboClone never reacts angrily to anything said to it by a living creature. Pip came through to the FoodSpace. She bent down to the cat.

'Please don't call me *the real one* in front of Pip 2,' she whispered, glancing at Pip 2. 'I don't think she likes it.'

Squeezy-Paws looked up at Pip 2. 'Hmm. I guess it does look kind of upset.'

'*Shh*!' said Pip. 'But, yes, you did tell me about your food. And I said you should eat KitABeef Product 67. Stop trying to trick Pip 2.'

Suddenly there was a loud bang from inside the lab. Pip looked over.

'What's going on?' she said.

'IT'S OKAY!' shouted Ivan.

'EVERYTHING'S FINE!' shouted Nina.

But then they started to do a lot of coughing and the small round window went black. Pip 2 immediately ran over with a cloth and reached up to try to clean it. Which was a bit silly because a) it wasn't dirt – it was smoke, and b) all the smoke was on the other side of the window. But

Pip 2 *was* a RoboClone that needed upgrading.

'Mum! Dad!' shouted Pip, trying to see past Pip 2.

'You are not allowed in the LabSpace,' said Pip 2, pushing her away.

'I know that! But—'

Pip 2 pushed her again, quite roughly. Once more Pip thought that was really odd: anger against humans was prohibited for a RoboClone, and of course violence even more so. Pip tapped her G-Glasses to try to MindLink with Pip 2 so she could figure out what was going on with the RoboClone—

But just then the LabSpace door opened, and a huge cloud of black smoke billowed out. Pip's mum and dad stumbled into the MainSpace, coughing and spluttering. Everything went very dark.

'Pip! Where are you?' shouted her mum.

'Here!' shouted Pip.

'Okay!' she said. 'I've got you!'

'Come this way!' shouted her dad. 'Don't worry! We'll just go and sit in another space and wait for the smoke to clear!

'Where will it go? Out of the window?' said Nina.

'Obviously not. We're not allowed to open them! Up the ventilation shafts. Meanwhile, let's get the pets and lock ourselves in our PodSpace!'

Scrabbling in the smoke, they made their way out of the MainSpace and into Nina and Ivan's PodSpace, and shut the door.

'Okay, good. Everyone here? Dag?'

'Yes.'

'Squeezy-Paws?'

'Meow.'

'Pip?'

'I've got Pip,' said Nina, who was still holding her hand.

'Yes, I'm here,' said Pip.

And Nina and Ivan were reassured because it certainly *sounded* like Pip.

CHAPTER 6

TRANSPORTER

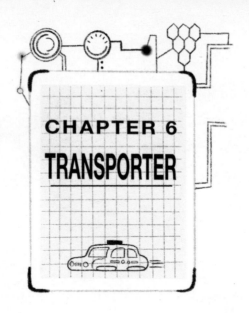

'Mum? Dad?' said Pip, who was lying on the floor, trying to breathe. She had hit the ground and stayed there when the black smoke came out of the lab, and had heard her parents calling for her . . . but then noticed that they'd stopped saying her name. It was weird.

At least it was becoming a bit easier to breathe. She looked up. The smoke had cleared enough for her to see where she was: in the LabSpace. She'd fallen into it.

'Mum? Da—' she said.

Then she thought: *Hmm. Maybe I'll stop calling for them. Just for a few minutes.* Because, even if Pip 2 was malfunctioning, the RoboClone had been right: Pip wasn't normally allowed in the LabSpace and she was curious about what was in there.

She got up and looked around. It was a small room, crowded with all sorts of things. In one corner, there was a HoverCabinet, marked **MEAL PILLS**. She opened it: inside were some small lozenges. *Hmm*, she thought. Maybe her mum and dad *were* trying to make 3020 more like people had thought it was going to be in the olden days after all! She tried one – it tasted like egg and soldiers! She smiled with pleasure and stuffed a handful of them into the pocket of her ImageSuit.

In another part of the LabSpace, there were lots of black boxes with switches on them. Some had built-in lights that were flashing on and off. Others had tiny screens with rapidly changing numbers on them. There were several crystals suspended in the air. One of the black boxes looked like it had exploded: the top had been ripped off, and Pip could see that this was where the smoke was coming from.

But she wasn't too worried about it: the smoke seemed to be dying down. And anyway she was more interested in what was behind that box. A large bright ring of green light seemed to be attached to the wall, but, on closer inspection, it was actually hovering a few centimetres away from it. There were two crystals on either side.

Pip peered into the ring and saw that the wall behind it simply wasn't there. There was only darkness, a completely black hole inside the circle of green light. She frowned, and reached up to touch the blackness – assuming it was some kind of illusion – and her hand went straight through it. More than that: she felt her hand being pulled *into* it.

Quickly, Pip took her hand out and backed away. *What* is *that*? she thought.

Underneath the ring was a HoverScreen, on which someone – probably her mum, who tended to do the maths – had scribbled a series of really complicated equations. Beneath those was the word **<u>TRANSPORTER</u>**, underlined.

'Oh!' said Pip. 'It's a Transport Portal!'

One problem with a world in which no one went outside was that humans did still sometimes have to get to other places, which weren't where they lived. The richer people had GravityLess Cars parked right outside their HouseUnits. They could go straight inside those through airlocks, and fly to wherever they needed to go without ever stepping outside. But most people either couldn't go out, or had to brave the frightening heat.

So some scientists were trying to invent a machine that could transport people from place to place, and from building to building, without them actually going outside. So far no one had managed to make it work. And there had also been one very messy incident involving a scientist and a fly.

But Pip's parents, it seemed, were still working on the problem.

Exciting, thought Pip, and it really was. She herself could not remember ever going outside. It felt so frustrating sometimes, having all this technology and only being able to use it indoors. *What's the point*, she often thought, *of having GravityLess Boots, and only ever using them to hover round the HouseUnit*?

She wished she could use them outdoors. She wished she could hover high above the towers, and feel the air on her face as she flew. Just for a few minutes.

Pip looked around, expecting to see another bright ring somewhere. Because, she thought, her parents must be testing the transporter in the lab, and probably, what you did, was to go into this ring and come out another one. But there wasn't another ring to be seen.

'Hmm,' she said. 'That's odd. Maybe it's in another part of the HouseUnit.'

It then occurred to Pip that she was never going to know the answer to this because her parents didn't allow her in the lab. So they'd never let her try out the transporter. This made Pip cross. *It's not fair,* she thought. *They get to try out all these amazing gadgets and I never get a go. I just have to stay in my pod and then be at school in the Learning Matrix, and listen to the cat and the parrot fight, while Mum and Dad get to do all the cool stuff.*

The other ring must be somewhere else in the HouseUnit, she reasoned. Or, more excitingly, somewhere else in the block. Or even, she thought, somewhere else in the City! Maybe she would come out at the Stadium Above the Clouds! She'd never been there in real life, of course – only the *very* rich could afford tickets to see games live at the stadium, and you needed a TurboCharged GravityLess Vehicle to get there. But, once you were inside, it was so high that it was one of the very few places left on Earth that wasn't hot, and no viruses could penetrate the sealed roof. You could watch a whole match without worrying!

By the time she'd finished thinking all this, Pip had convinced herself that this was *definitely* where the other ring was: that, if you stepped into the portal on the wall, you would instantly come out of another one in the Stadium Above the Clouds.

People do that sometimes. They wish the world was a certain way and so they decide that, yes, it *is* like that.

I'll only have a quick look, thought Pip. *Just at the view from the Executive Pods. Then I'll turn round and come back straight away*.

And, with that thought, she raised herself up, took a deep breath and climbed through the bright green ring into darkness.

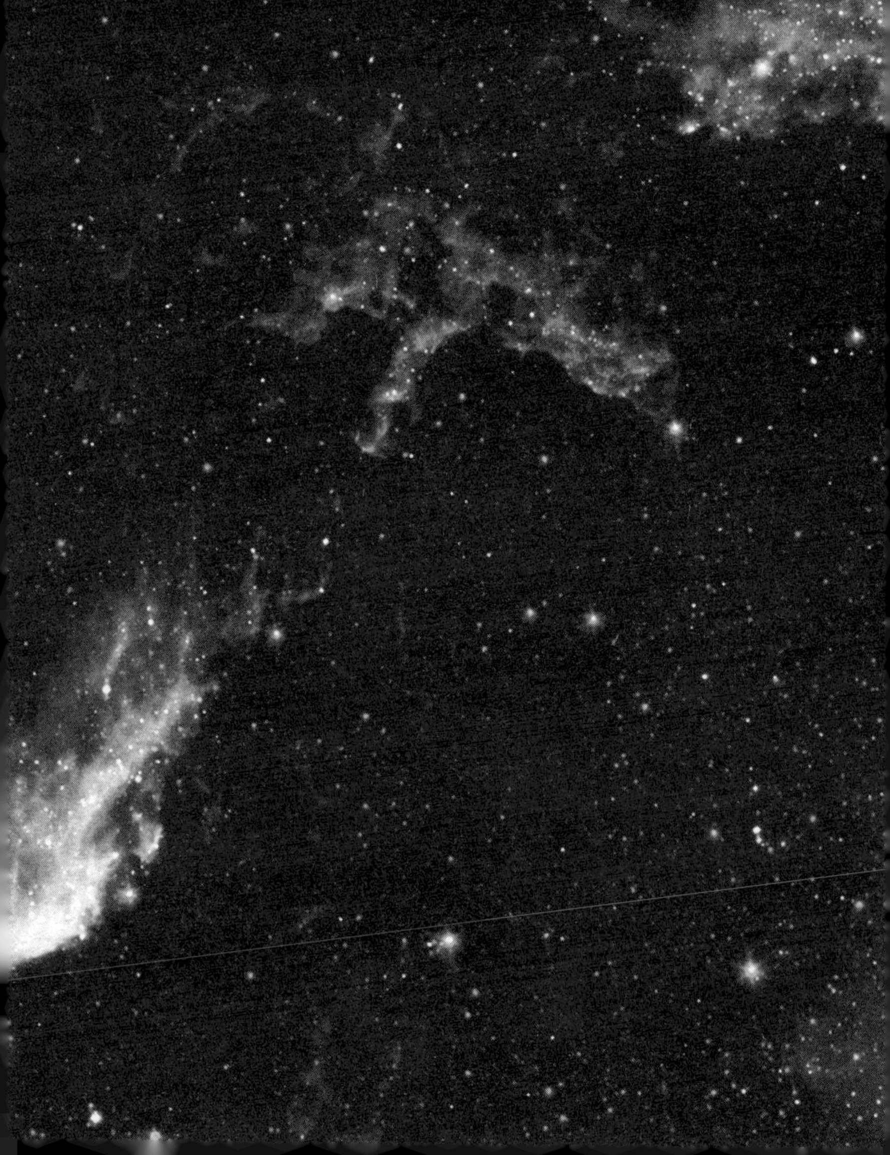

2019

CHAPTER 7
Whatever You're Looking For, We've Got it . . . Somewhere

It was Sunday, so Rahul Agarwal and his family were watching that TV show where people bring in antiques for experts to look at. A man with a beard was nodding at an expert in a bow tie, who was holding a vase and talking.

'Look at him,' said Rahul's dad, Sanjay. 'Look at his eyes. So bored. So full of, "Please stop explaining where it's from – just TELL ME WHAT IT'S WORTH!"'

Sanjay looked over at Rahul, who normally

laughed when he said this (which he did *every* time the show was on). But Rahul just carried on watching blankly.

'Come on, Rahul!' said Sanjay. 'Cheer up!'

'I'm fine, Dad.'

'Are you sure?' said his mum, looking up from the TV. Prisha was sitting in her favourite chair, the one underneath the large framed photo of her Uncle Raj.

'Don't ask me about my homework,' said Rahul.

'Who said anything about homework?' said Sanjay.

'That's what Mum always means,' said Rahul. 'When she asks me *anything*.'

'I beg your pardon?' said Prisha.

'"How are you feeling, Rahul?" means: have you done your homework? "Have you had a good day, Rahul?" means: have you done your homework? So I assume "are you sure?" means: have you done your homework?'

'That is very unfair, Rahul. Isn't it, Sanjay?'

Sanjay blinked.

'I said, *isn't it, Sanjay*?'

'Um . . . anyway, Rahul, why don't you go and invent something? You haven't done that for ages!'

Sanjay was right. Some of you who read my last book might remember that Rahul liked to invent things. His greatest invention was a wheelchair that he turned into a supercar, and that his friend Amy Taylor had driven, with him in the passenger seat, all the way to Scotland.

But, since then, that car had fallen to pieces (on a race track in Scotland). And, although Rahul was proud of having made the Taylor TurboChaser, he felt that with it he'd taken inventing as far as he could. Which meant that now he'd sort of . . . retired.

Plus, Amy was spending much more time with her dad in Scotland, so although Rahul was pleased that he had helped her – a lot – he also felt a bit sad sometimes. Because he'd ended up losing his best friend.

'I don't really have invention ideas any more,' he said.

'Hmm,' said Sanjay, looking worried. He was genuinely concerned, as he was of the firm belief that, one day, Rahul was going to invent something that would mean he didn't have to work quite so hard every day. 'Don't say that. You'll come up with something.'

Rahul didn't say anything.

'Why don't you just go and have a look through all the gear downstairs? That's how you usually get ideas.'

Sanjay owned a big warehouse called Agarwal Supplies, which the family lived above. He was right. In the past, all of Rahul's inventions had come from using stuff he found in there. Which fitted with the sign above the warehouse:

**Whatever You're Looking For,
We've Got It . . . Somewhere!**

Although that sign had now gone missing.

'I dunno, Dad,' said Rahul, shaking his head. 'I'm really not sure I'm cut out to be an inventor any more . . .'

His dad clearly didn't know what to say. He looked very sad.

'Oh well!' said Prisha. 'If you're *not* going to be thinking about silly inventions, maybe you can sit down at the table and make sure you do your homew—'

'I'll just go and have a look in the warehouse,' said Rahul, getting up.

CHAPTER 8
Inflatable dartboard

Rahul sat on a beanbag – one of twenty, in all different colours – in the warehouse. One of his favourite planned inventions, in the past, had been bean pants, which would allow the wearer to have the sensation of sitting on a beanbag, but without the bag.

In the old days, he would've been prodding the beanbag to work out exactly what type of beans were in there, how many you would need per pair of pants, and then maybe going over to the hundreds of pants boxed up in the far corner to work out exactly how to sew an internal lining in them to hold the beans.

But today he was just sitting on the beanbag, looking at his phone. He wasn't even jotting down ideas in his favourite notebook (seeing the last one – **inflatable dartboard** – only made him feel more depressed). He was just scrolling through some old messages from Amy, thinking about how much he missed her, and wondering if he'd stayed down here long enough for his dad to think he'd been inventing, when he heard a noise.

He looked up. It was a strange noise, a kind of whooshing, like it was windy outside and a window had been left open in the warehouse. Except it wasn't a windy day.

Rahul got up from the beanbag (with a bit

of difficulty – it was a big one and he was quite squashed into it).

'Hello?' he said.

No one replied. But the whooshing sound continued. He walked round to where it seemed to be coming from, which was somewhere near the extra-large toilet seats and the boxes of cough mixture that they weren't allowed to sell any more.

'Hello?' he said again. The whooshing sound, he now realised, was accompanied by a bumping noise.

Bump. Bump. Bump.

Rahul walked over to that part of the warehouse. The whooshing and bumping got louder, but he couldn't see anyone. All he saw was the row of extra-large toilet seats, none of which anyone had bought, even though Sanjay had been totally convinced that, with the amount people ate these days, they'd be selling like hot cakes.

'Like the hot cakes people are eating so many

of these days, Rahul!' he'd added while Rahul had helped him stack them up against the wall.

But then Rahul looked more closely. In the middle of the row of toilet seats, there was one where the lid was not properly shut. Which was not particularly noticeable in itself – but what *was* strange was that it seemed to be . . . moving. The lid was banging up and down . . . as if someone was trying to open it from behind.

Which was odd, as all that was behind it was the warehouse wall. But not quite as odd as the fact that the rim of the toilet seat was lit up in a bright green oval ring.

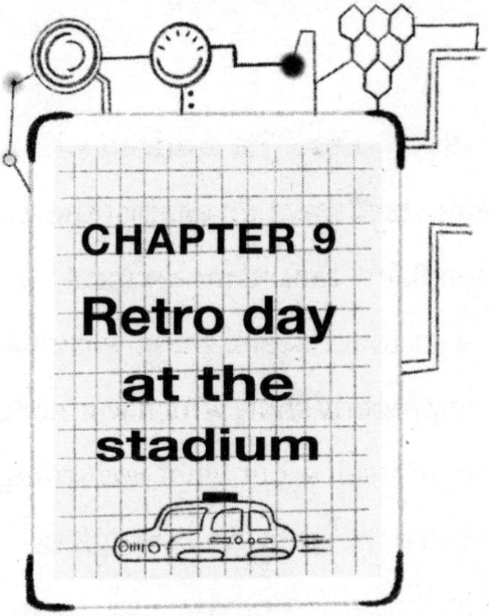

CHAPTER 9

Retro day at the stadium

Rahul thought about screaming. It was a strange moment because screaming – well, you might think that's something that you do straight away, as soon as you're frightened. You don't stop to think about it.

But actually Rahul – who was a thoughtful fellow – *was* thinking about it. He was thinking: *Oh my Lord, I'm frightened*. But also, What *is going on here*? His curiosity, in other words, was battling against his fear and eventually it overcame it.

He didn't scream. He peered down at the toilet seat, and put his hand on the edge of the lid. As his fingers gripped it, he muttered a short prayer: *Please, whatever else comes out of here, please let it not be a huge wave of ghost poo*.

And, with that prayer sent up to no one in particular, he pulled on the lid. It was easier to open than he expected. It was, in fact, about as easy to open as a toilet lid normally is; somehow he'd expected it was going to be much harder. Rahul was relieved that no ghost poo came out.

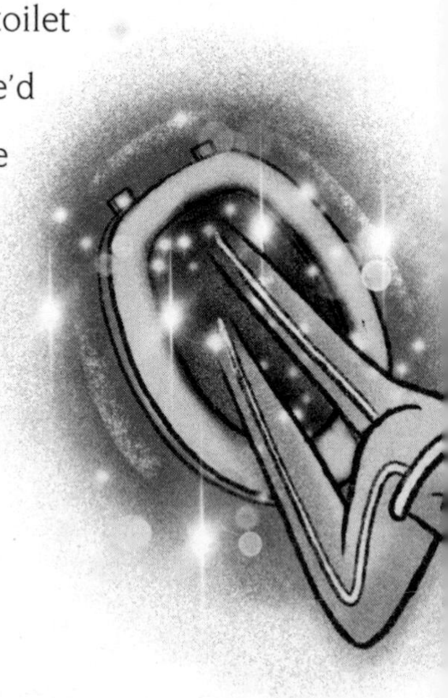

But he did scream this time because what did emerge from the toilet seat was a girl.

'AAAARRGGGH!' said Rahul, backing away fast.

The girl tumbled out and rolled over a couple of times. Then she sat up.

'AAARGGGHH!' said Rahul again.

'Hello,' said the girl. 'Are you all right?'

'WHAT! AARGH! NO! YOU'VE JUST APPEARED OUT OF A TOILET!'

The girl frowned and looked round. 'No, that's a portal.'

'NO, IT'S A TOILET! WELL, A SEAT! WITH A LID!'

Rahul started to think these were slightly strange words to be shouting. So he tried to calm himself down, in order to speak more quietly. But she spoke first.

'No,' said the girl, going over to it. 'It's definitely a portal. It's got the ring of green light. And besides, obviously, we don't have toilets any more. Our waste is just processed remotely and turned directly into biofuel. Not that it's really helped the environment.'

Rahul shook his head and frowned. 'Right, well, all those words were just noise. *It's a toilet seat.*'

The girl looked at it again. 'No. It can't be. Apart from anything, it's much too big for any normal person's bottom!'

She moved away from the toilet seat and looked around. 'Is this the back entrance to the stadium?'

'Pardon me?'

'Or maybe the changing rooms?'

'Sorry? What stadium?'

The girl laughed and said, as if it was obvious,

'The Stadium Above the Clouds!'

Rahul frowned. 'Um . . . is that a song?'

Now the girl frowned. 'I don't think so. But there might be one about it.'

Rahul came closer. She was quite a strange-looking girl. She had short hair, cut in an odd style he'd never seen before, as if she'd asked her hairdresser to shave it close, but leave little pyramids of hair sticking up all over her scalp. And her clothes were . . . *weird*. She was wearing a shiny silver one-piece suit, made out of plastic or Lycra or something, but it didn't seem to have any zips or buttons. There was one pocket, but not on the side, in the middle.

'What on earth are you *wearing*?' she asked.

'Um . . .' said Rahul. 'I was just about to ask *you* that.'

'Is it some kind of retro day at the stadium? Like, are you part of a history parade or something?'

Rahul shook his head. 'I really don't know what

this stadium thing you're going on about is. This is just my T-shirt. Look. What's your name?'

The girl frowned again. 'Hasn't it come up in your G-Glasses?'

'My what?' said Rahul.

'Your G-Glasses. My name should come up as soon as you scan me.'

Rahul took his glasses off and looked at them. 'I got these at Specsavers.'

'Hmm,' said the girl. 'Well, anyway, my name is Pip@256X#YY.3_7.'

'Pardon?' said Rahul.

'Pip@256X#YY.3_7.'

'Yeah,' said Rahul. 'And mine is Rahul@bbc.co.uk.'

The girl nodded. 'Pleased to meet you.'

'No, it isn't really.'

'What?'

'That *isn't* my name. I was joking. Goodness! *I'm* the one people normally say doesn't get jokes.'

The girl squinted at him. She reached into her pocket and took out a pair of glasses. She put them on and Rahul saw lights come on round the frame. The girl stared at him, moving her eyes up and down.

'That's odd,' she said. 'You don't have any readings. Have you gone off-MindLink?'

'Look,' said Rahul, 'my name is Rahul Agarwal. And this is my dad's warehouse, Agarwal Supplies!'

The girl took off her glasses. 'It's not the Stadium Above the Clouds?'

Rahul shook his head. 'I don't know where that is. But this is really not it. Apart from anything, we aren't above the clouds. We're very much on the ground. If you look out there, you'll see the A41. And two chicken shops.'

'Oh no!' said the girl, looking suddenly worried. 'Am I in Zone X? Are the chickens armed?'

'Er . . . dunno about arms,' said Rahul. 'I think you

can definitely have *legs*. If you order a Big Bucket.'

The girl looked troubled. 'Right, I think maybe I should just go back home.'

'Um . . .' said Rahul. 'Okay. But . . . how? It's really late. Are your mum and dad going to come and pick you up?'

'What?' said Pip. 'No. I'll just go back through the portal . . .'

'The . . .'

'Look, it was nice to meet you, but . . . goodbye.'

She went back to the lit-up toilet seat and lifted the lid. Rahul noticed for the first time that, through the seat, he couldn't see the wall of the warehouse. Instead, inside the ring, there was just a vast blackness. And a whooshing sound. That was where it had been coming from!

OMG, thought Rahul, *maybe it is a . . . a portal!*

'Wait a moment . . .' he said. 'Where exactly are you from? What did you mean about not having toilets *any more*? About me looking like I'm in a *history* parade?'

'Sorry, but I think I have to go,' said the girl, preparing to dive into the toilet seat. 'I don't know how much longer the portal will stay open.'

'Wait!' said Rahul. 'Pip!'

On hearing her name spoken for the first time – it was actually the first time Pip had heard her name said by someone outside her HouseUnit ever – she looked round.

She smiled at Rahul slightly sadly, as if to say: *I'd love to, but I can't*. And then turned back to jump into the blackness.

At which point, a parrot came flying out of the toilet seat and hit her in the face.

CHAPTER 10

THE CHICKENS HAVE SURRENDERED!

'FREE! FREE AT LAST! FREE TO FLY LIKE THE BIRD I AM! LIKE THE BIRD I WAS ALWAYS MEANT TO BE!' screeched the parrot, flying round and round the warehouse. It was veering dangerously close to the tinned hot dogs.

'A PARROT HAS COME OUT OF THE TOILET SEAT!' shouted Rahul. Then he shook his head. 'I can't believe I said those words! Am I going mad?'

'It's not a toilet seat!' said Pip, rubbing her face.

'It's a portal!'

'A portaloo?'

'What? No! A Transporter Portal! Dag! DAG!' she shouted.

'I told you, my name's Rahul!'

'I'm not talking to you! DAG!'

'LET ME BE, PIP! LET ME FLY!'

Rahul stared up at the parrot. 'Is it . . . talking to you?'

'TO FLY LIKE A BIRD, LIKE A BIRD ON THE WING . . .' sang the parrot operatically.

'DAG!' Pip stuck her hand out and blinked twice. The parrot's flight immediately spun away from the tinned sausages towards the large sacks of firelighters, and it came to Pip, settling on her hand.

'Blast!' said the parrot. 'I forgot about my homing chip!'

'Yes, well, you've had a nice long fly-around now. You shouldn't have flown into the portal, but, if you behave yourself, I won't tell Mum and Dad. It's time to go home.'

Rahul stared. 'That's an amazing parrot. I've never seen one that can talk like that before.'

'Excuse me!' said Dag. 'I AM here. Right in front of you.'

'Incredible,' said Rahul. 'It's like it really understands what we're saying.'

The parrot shook its beak from side to side. 'Rude. Just rude.'

'Anyway,' said Pip, 'we really have to go!'

Still holding the parrot, she bent down towards the toilet seat.

'Hmm,' she said. 'The lid's fallen shut.'

'That's okay,' said Rahul. 'It was easy to open before.'

Pip pulled at it. 'Not now it isn't.'

Rahul frowned. 'Let me have a go.' He crouched down and curled his fingers round the lid, then tried to move his hands backwards. It wouldn't budge.

'Hmm. It's probably just a bad hinge.'

'No,' said Pip, sounding very worried. 'I think the portal's shut. Locked!'

'What does *that* mean?' said Rahul.

'It means I can't use it get back to Zone J. Where I live.' Pip shook her head. 'I don't know what to do. I suppose I could contact Mum and Dad and explain what happened . . .'

'They'll be cross,' said Dag, nodding his beak up and down.

'They will. And, when they have to pay for a GravityLess Taxi to get me back, they'll be even crosser . . .'

'Haven't they got GravityLess Uber here?' asked Dag.

At this point, a thought that had been trickling for a while in Rahul's head became a torrent.

'Excuse me,' he said. 'I think you need to understand something. If . . . I have understood something. Correctly.'

'What?' said Pip.

'Yes?' said Dag.

Rahul cleared his throat. 'What year is it?'

Pip frowned. 'Weird question.'

'Yeah,' said Dag. 'Haven't you set the date and time in your G-Glasses? Or MindLink? I know a lot of people never do and just leave them at 0/0/0000.'

'Sorry,' said Rahul, 'but can you just answer the question?'

Pip shrugged. 'It's 3020, of course!'

Rahul nodded and got out his phone.

Pip laughed. Dag made a strange screeching noise, which was probably him laughing too.

'Man!' said Dag. 'What is *that*! Is that like . . . something from that ScreenHive show? You know, Pip – the one where people bring in old stuff and experts go on about it and you just *know* the people only want to be told how much it's worth!'

'Is that still on in 3020?' said Rahul. 'Blimey. Anyway, would you mind just looking at what it says on the screen?'

Pip stopped laughing and looked. 'It seems to be a picture of you and some girl in a chair with wheels on . . . ?'

'Yes. But what does it say *above* that? Underneath the time of day?'

Pip peered into it. 'The eleventh of October—' She stopped and looked up.

'2019!' said Dag. 'Well, you want to get *that* fixed. Obviously, an antique like that is bound to go wrong.'

'It's not wrong,' said Rahul. 'Phone, what date is it?'

His phone made a whirring noise. '*I found a number of Italian restaurants close to you. Would you like me to list them*?'

Pip laughed again and Dag did that screeching thing.

'Oh my days,' said Rahul. 'You're useless.' He looked back at the girl and the parrot. 'It *is* 2019. Look, we can go outside and *ask* someone!'

Pip stopped laughing. Dag stopped screeching.

'We can . . . do what?' said Pip.

'Go outside.'

Rahul walked over to the side wall where there was a window covered by a flowery curtain (originally meant for a shower, but cut to fit the window by Prisha). He opened the curtain.

Through the window was a view of the road. There were cars on it and a few people walking – and indeed two chicken shops, in which some other people were probably waiting for Big Buckets.

Pip and Dag looked through the window.

'You know what this means, don't you?' said Dag.

'Yes,' said Pip, who had gone white.

'THE CHICKENS HAVE SURRENDERED!'

said Dag.

Pip shook her head. 'No, Dag. It means the portal we just came through wasn't a transporter.' She shook her head again, as if she couldn't quite believe it herself. 'It was a *Time—*'

'RAHUL!' shouted Prisha, coming into the warehouse. 'Where are you? Why have you been skulking in here for so long! RAHUL!'

'Oh no!' said Rahul. 'Quick! Hide!'

Pip nodded, blinked and disappeared.

CHAPTER 11

Pretty Polly! Pretty Polly!

Back in their living room, Prisha was very cross. Not about Rahul spending a long time in the warehouse. About Dag.

Who was presently perched on Rahul's shoulder.

'Urrgh! Where did you get it from?'

'It just . . . flew into the warehouse. I . . . don't know where from,' said Rahul. (All of which was, in fact, true.)

'Well,' said Prisha, 'you can't keep it!'

'Enough of the it, if you please, madam!' said Dag. 'I am not a robot. I am a man parrot! A very manly parrot!'

'He speaks so well!' said Sanjay. 'Impressive!'

'Thank you, good sir,' said Dag. 'I try my best to use only the words and grammar that befit a gentleman parrot of my standing.'

'Amazing,' said Sanjay. 'Hey! Maybe we could rent him out! To a circus!'

'I beg your pardon?' said Dag.

'Oh, shush, Sanjay,' said Prisha. 'I'm not having a bird in the house!'

They started arguing. Loudly.

During which time, Rahul moved into the hall, and

whispered to Dag: 'So . . . parrots have evolved to speak as well as humans in your time?'

'I would say *better* than most humans,' said Dag. 'Actually, so have most animals.'

'Goodness.'

'Not frogs, though.'

'Right.'

'They still just croak.'

'Okay . . . amazing . . .'

'It hasn't always been for the good. The chickens, fed up with the way they were treated for years by humans, have become very militant. That's been quite difficult for everyone. And . . .'

'Um, Dag. That's your name, right?'

'Yes.'

'Bit strange. Not Percy?'

Dag stared at him. 'I come from a thousand and one years in the future. I can speak. Properly. So, parrot-name-wise, things have moved on from *Percy*.'

'Right, right. Of course. Listen, I think maybe you should . . . tone it down a bit. The speaking. Otherwise they'll get suspicious.'

'*Tone it down a bit*?'

'Yeah. Be a bit less . . . clever.'

Dag shook his head. 'That's a tough one for me. I pride myself on my cleverness.'

'Try. Meanwhile, where's Pip? She just vanished.'

'Here,' said a voice.

'Who said that?'

'Pip,' said Dag in a bored way.

'Yes,' said the voice.

Rahul looked round. 'But where from? Where are you hiding? I thought you were still in the warehouse!

'No, I followed you in here.'

'Where ARE you?'

'I'm right in front of you.'

'She's wearing an ImageSuit. Presently set to *Invisible*,' said Dag. 'Oh sorry, am I being too *clever*?'

'Really?' said Rahul excitedly. 'You're invisible?'

'Yes!' said Pip's voice. 'But I don't want to be for much longer. It uses a lot of power, and I don't even know how – or if – I can recharge my suit here . . .'

'So, Rahul,' said Sanjay, appearing at the living-room door, with Prisha glowering behind. 'Your mother's right. We can't keep the bird. It probably belongs to someone anyway. We need to find out who that is . . .'

'Okay, Dad. Well, look, let's keep him for today, and I'll start trying to find out who his owner is tomorrow.'

'Oh, for heaven's sake! Can't we just . . . throw

him out of the window and let him fly away?' said Prisha.

'No, Mum!' said Rahul. 'I . . . I don't think he'll find his way home.'

'Of course he will!' said Prisha, reaching for Rahul's shoulder. 'Look, I'll just take him and—'

There was a crash. Everyone turned back to the living room. Where the picture of Uncle Raj had fallen off the wall.

'OH NO!' cried Prisha. 'Uncle Raj!'

Sanjay looked at her. 'It happened when you reached for the parrot.' His face was serious, as if he was saying, *So therefore it was an omen*. 'Maybe we should let him stay. For the moment.'

'Hmm,' said Prisha, bending down to pick up the picture. The glass in the frame had shattered. 'Well, as long as it's not because you're planning to rent him out as the Amazing Talking Bird!'

'Of course not!' As his wife went into the kitchen

to get a dustpan and brush, he added, with a wink, 'Eh, clever parrot?'

'Pretty Polly! Pretty Polly! Pretty Pol!' said Dag.

'Hmm,' said Sanjay. 'There goes that idea. Okay, I'll go and see if we've got a cage in the warehouse.'

As he went out, Dag said: '*Stupid* enough for you?'

'Yes,' said Rahul. 'Pip? Are you here?'

'Hello, yes,' said Pip's voice from over by the wall. 'Sorry about Uncle Raj, but I had to do something.'

CHAPTER 12

Just a real blink

The three of them – Pip, Dag and Rahul – went up to Rahul's room. Although anyone else would have just seen a boy and a parrot.

'So, listen,' said Pip, 'can we—'

'No,' said Rahul. 'I'm not talking to nothing.'

There was a tut, then Pip shimmered into view.

'Wow!' said Rahul.

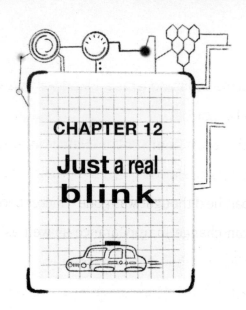

'It's really not that impressive,' said Pip. 'An internal quantum computer just creates an electronic casing around me which deflects all light waves away from my body.'

'Right,' said Rahul, not completely understanding, but interested. He could feel the inventor part of him – the part he'd thought was gone – flicker back to life.

'It can change in appearance as well as become invisible.'

'Really?'

'Yes! Because it's synced up to the visual cortex in my brain. All I have to do is focus on what I'd *like* to look like –' she shut her eyes – 'and then blink, activating my internal MindLink . . .'

She shimmered again. The silver ImageSuit was replaced, in the shimmer, by . . . a football kit! It was blue shorts with a gold top. A bit like the kit Brazil wear now, except the gold shone very brightly. It looked like actual gold.

'Wow!' said Rahul. 'Whose kit is that?'

'It's my team. The City Cardinals!'

He squinted at her top. 'Is that . . . real gold . . . ?'

'No, Rahul. I'm still wearing the ImageSuit, remember? But, yes, the team's top is made by scientists who mix the molecular structure of gold with nylon.' She blinked and the standard silver ImageSuit returned.

'So . . . people still play football? Like we do?'

'Of course! Well, actually, I'm not sure. Do your teams use GravityLess Boots?'

'What?'

'These!' said Pip and shot up in the air. 'Ow!' she said, as she banged her head on the ceiling. She hovered back down again. 'I forgot your RoomSpaces are smaller than ours . . .'

Rahul stared at her. 'This is *incredible*,' he said.

'Is it? Everyone has this stuff in our time. In fact, you can get much, much more exciting ImageSuits and GravityLess Boots than these.'

'Excuse me!' said Dag, flying between them and settling on the edge of Rahul's bed. 'Can we talk, please? About what's happened here?'

'Yes,' said Rahul. 'Can we?'

'Well,' said Pip. 'Yes. Except I don't know myself for sure.'

Rahul sat down next to Dag. 'Okay. So what *do* we know?'

Pip thought. 'This morning me and Dag were in 3020. Then we went through a portal and now we're in 2019. We've gone back a thousand and one years!'

'Right. Okay. And the portal, for the moment, is shut. Why is that?'

Pip shook her head. 'I'm not sure. I didn't even think it was a Time Portal when I went into it. I thought it was just a transporter one. I thought it would take me to . . .' And here she blushed a little.

'The Stadium Above the Clouds,' said Rahul. 'Is that where the City Cardinals play?'

'Yes,' said Pip quietly. 'I've never actually been there. We can't afford tickets.' She sighed. 'I've never really been anywhere. I'm not allowed out of our HouseUnit.'

Rahul frowned. 'You've got boots that allow you to fly basically and you've *never* been outside?'

She nodded.

'I just practise with them inside. Most people can't go outdoors in our time. It's too hot. And there's lots of floods and viruses.'

'Don't you get bored, cooped up in your . . . HouseUnit all the time?'

'I guess,' said Pip. 'That's probably why I got so excited about the transporter taking me . . . somewhere else.'

She blinked.

'Oh,' said Rahul, after a moment.

'What?'

'I thought something was gonna happen then. Like you going invisible. Or an elephant appearing out of my cupboard. Because you blinked.'

'No, that was just a real blink. It only works when I imagine what I want to happen at the same time. That activates the MindLink.'

Rahul nodded. 'Your parents . . . won't they be missing you?'

'Well,' said Dag, 'when I flew away from them, they hadn't noticed you'd gone.'

'They hadn't?' said Pip, frowning.

'No. Because of Pip 2.'

'What?' said Pip.

'Who's that?' said Rahul.

'A RoboClone of me.'

'Um. Right. I see.'

'So,' said Dag, 'if I might continue . . . when the lab explosion happened, they grabbed hold of *its* hand. And then I noticed . . . well . . . that it was kind of pretending it WAS you.'

'What? Why?'

Dag shook his head and his feathers ruffled across

his scalp. 'I don't know. But I think your parents don't realise you've gone. Because they think Pip 2 *is* you.'

Pip stared at the parrot.

'I'm guessing from your expression that isn't good . . . ?' said Rahul.

'No,' said Pip. 'I don't think it sounds good at all. In fact, it sounds like I need to get home.'

CHAPTER 13

THE All-Weather Brella

'Okay,' said Rahul, 'here's my plan. We must get that portal open so you can get home. But first we need to keep who you are a secret.'

'Why?' asked Pip.

'Because, if the grown-ups find out you're from the future, they'll take you away for . . . testing and stuff. And you'll have to spend all your time with politicians and scientists, explaining to them all about the future.'

'That doesn't sound like much fun,' said Pip. 'And, what's more, I'll *never* get home.'

'I quite like the sound of it!' said Dag.

'Yeah, well, I don't think *you'll* be with the politicians and scientists. You'll be in a circus, rented out by my dad. Or possibly on a reality show on Channel Five.'

'Oh,' said Dag. 'That does *not* sound fun.'

'What's this?' said Pip.

Rahul turned round. She was holding up an enormous pair of men's Y-fronts.

'Um . . .' said Rahul, 'one of my inventions.'

'You're an inventor?'

'Well. Yes. I was.'

Pip stared at the enormous pair of pants. 'What is it?'

Rahul looked at Pip, in her ImageSuit that could make her look like anything she wanted to, and her GravityLess Boots that let her soar high in the air, and said: 'Um . . . bean pants?'

'Bean . . . sorry?'

'They're my dad's old underpants.' Pip made a grossed-out face, but Rahul said: 'Don't worry. They're clean. He hasn't worn them for years. They've got beans sewn into them. Dried ones, not baked obviously. Baked would drip tomato sauce.'

Pip held up a hand and gingerly touched the back of the pants.

'Yes, I can feel . . . some beans. I think.'

'They make it feel like you're sitting on a beanbag.'

'*O-kay* . . .' said Pip.

'Do you know what a beanbag is?'

'No.'

'Do you want to try them?' said Rahul.

'Not really.'

'Fair enough.'

'Have you invented anything else?'

'Loads of things. There's this . . .' He went over to

the cupboard and took out an umbrella.

'What's that?' said Pip.

'It's an umbrella. But not just any umbrella . . . it's an All-Weather Brella!' He opened it with a flourish.

Pip nodded. 'I don't know what an umbrella is,' she said.

'It stops you getting wet,' said Rahul, 'when it rains. But –' he pointed to a small plastic flap in the top of the brolly – 'I added this window, you see, so if it's rainy and sunny, like it sometimes is, you can have the best of both worlds . . .'

'Oh,' said Pip. 'In 3020, it rains really hard, and when it's not raining it's so hot that I'm not sure that would work.'

'Right. Well, I made a wheelchair into a car as well, but . . . I can't show you that.'

'Is this it?' said Pip. She had picked up a notebook, which had been underneath the All-Weather Brella. It had the words MY INVENTIONS written on it.

'Yes,' said Rahul. He flicked it open. On the middle page was the original design for the Taylor TurboChaser, with lots of words scribbled on it as well, like . . .

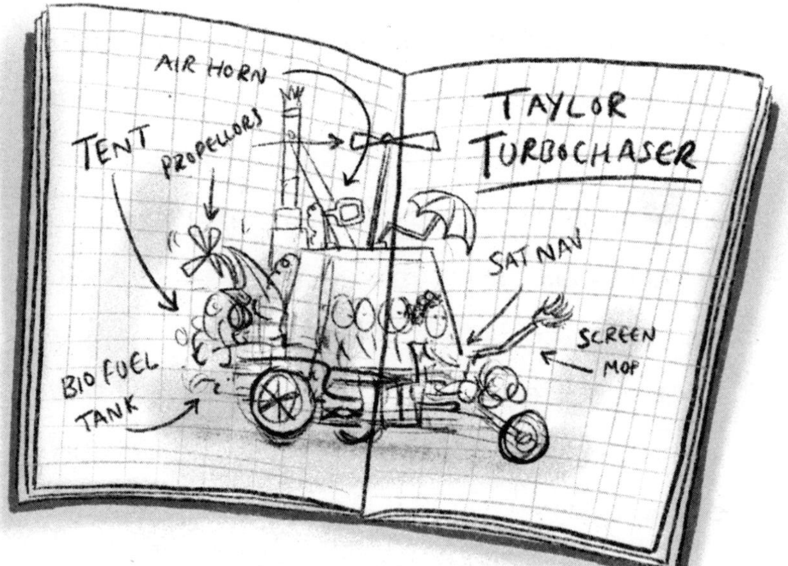

'It looks amazing,' Pip said.

'Thank you,' said Rahul. 'It kind of was.'

'But, hey! Maybe this – maybe *you* – are the way back!'

'Pardon?'

'Well, you're an inventor! A scientist! Surely you can invent a way of getting me back to 3020!'

Rahul frowned. 'Um . . . I think maybe bean pants and the All-Weather Brella – even an electric wheelchair made into a car – are a bit less complicated than a portal to 3020.'

'Are they?' said Pip. 'The portal's already there anyway – it's just a question of getting it open!'

Rahul looked at her. She was smiling at him with excitement. He shook his head.

'I don't know,' he said, sitting down on the bed. He put the notebook back in the cupboard. 'I really don't. I've kind of . . . given up inventing anyway.'

'Have you?' said Pip. 'Why?'

Rahul sighed. 'It's a long story. I just have.'

Pip looked at Dag.

Dag shrugged and said: 'Awks.'

'Do you mean squawk?' said Rahul, not turning round.

'Hey!' said Pip. 'This is brilliant!'

'What is?'

'Look!'

Pip was sitting on the floor. In the bean pants. 'It's so comfy! Who knew? It's so like sitting on a beanbag!'

Rahul laughed. 'But you don't even know what that's like!'

Pip shook her head. 'I do now!' She stood up. 'You're a brilliant inventor!'

The pants fell down. Which made Rahul laugh again.

'Okay, okay,' he said. 'I'll have a think about it!'

'Excellent!' said Pip.

CHAPTER 14

So silver

'But first of all,' said Rahul, 'we'll need to find a way of keeping you secret here. You could hide in the warehouse, but I'll be at school for most of the day tomorrow, and my dad goes in there – the warehouse, I mean – a lot . . .'

'What if I come to school with you?' said Pip.

'You *want* to go to school?' said Rahul.

'Yes! It's exciting for me. We only go to school on the Grid.'

'The Grid – is that like the internet?'

'Yes! That's what Miss Lucy *said* it used to be called!'

'Miss . . . ?'

'My history teacher.'

'I thought you didn't go to school?'

'It's a virtual school called the Learning Matrix. It's inside the Grid. Hey! Does your school have – what did Miss Lucy say they were called – a *playground*?'

'Well. Yeah. Kind of.'

Pip looked very excited. 'A football pitch?'

Rahul smiled. 'Yeah, we play football on it, but it's more waste ground than playground really . . . I'd dial down your expectations a bit when it comes to Bracket Wood. Anyway, Pip, these clothes . . .'

He turned to his wardrobe and pulled out an outfit.

'Now that really does look like something from a history parade,' said Pip.

'Very funny. It's my school uniform. Can you get the ImageSuit to do a version of yourself in these? A girl's version, of course . . . ?'

'What's a *girl's* version?' said Pip, frowning. 'In 3020, boys and girls don't wear different clothes.'

'Um . . .'

'Never mind. I'll just try a version that I think will work for me.'

She put on her G-Glasses. She scanned Rahul up and down (which made him – not someone who thought of himself as male-model material – feel a bit self-conscious). Then she nodded to herself and blinked twice.

The shimmering happened again. The ImageSuit became Pip in Bracket Wood school uniform. Except it was also a bodysuit, like a superhero's costume, and still silver: so silver that Rahul could see his reflection in it. It was like something you'd get if you crossbred the Bracket Wood school uniform with an outfit worn by one of the Avengers.

Pip posed in it, hand on hip.

'Yeah,' said Rahul. 'I think that *might* draw a bit of attention to you at school.'

Pip shrugged. 'Okay, we can tone it down a bit when we actually go. What do you think, Dag?'

'Pretty Pippy! Pretty Pippy!' said Dag. 'Hey, I'm getting good at this!'

PART TWO

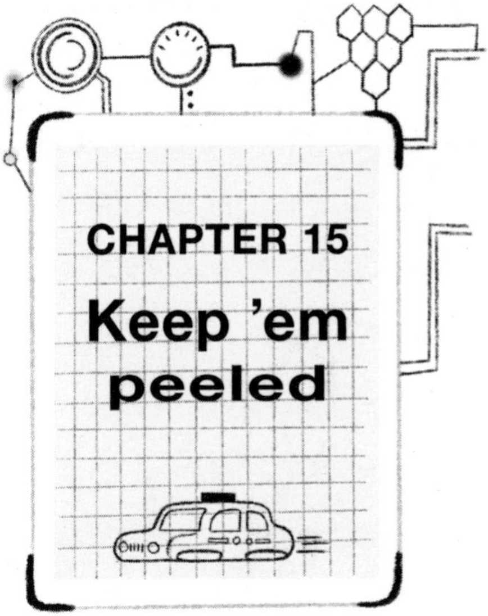

CHAPTER 15
Keep 'em peeled

Frank Flackle didn't really think his son, Gunther, should go to school. As far as Frank was concerned, Gunther could learn everything he needed to know at home. From Frank. And from the internet, which was where Frank had learned most things that he knew to be absolutely true about life.

Frank knew, for example – absolutely – that the Earth was flat. All those scientists you saw on the telly saying it was round were lying. They'd been paid by dark, world-controlling forces. Frank could never explain quite what these were, but he knew THEY were there, doing their dark world-controlling – to fool the gullible public. Frank knew THEY were covering up how many people, every day, were falling off the edge of the planet. This was why he always insisted that his family never went on holiday further than sixty miles from home.

'You can't be too careful, Nicola,' he'd say to his wife, who would nod obediently, and not say very much, as she set up the family tent in a field near Swindon.

He knew, as well, that the moon landings never happened: they had been faked by the American government under instructions from the dark, world-controlling forces. He had studied the footage very carefully on his favourite website, SecretOPedia, and was keen to point out, to Gunther, all the bits that gave the faking away.

'See, Gunther?' he would say. 'If you look closely, you'll see that the flag that the –' and here he would mime some inverted commas – '"astronaut" is planting on the –' he did them again – '"moon" is *waving*. And what tiny mistake have they made there, sonny?'

'There's no wind on the moon, Dad!'

'And what does that mean, son?'

'It means the whole thing was filmed in a studio somewhere. Where someone had left a door open. And there was a draught!'

At which point, Frank's eyes would grow moist, and he would hug his son and say, 'That's my boy.'

But Gunther *did* have to go to school. That was the law. The law, of course, was made by THEM, the dark, world-controlling forces. In fact, THEY had sent some people round from social services a few months ago to say that if Gunther wasn't seen at school soon Frank and Nicola would be in big trouble.

As it happened, Gunther had already been in big trouble himself at his previous school because of his attempts to convince other children of some of his handed-down-from-his-dad opinions. Unfortunately, Gunther didn't tend to use his brain – such as it was – in these arguments so much as his fists. One nerdy boy who tried to explain to Gunther that the world definitely wasn't flat had ended up upside down in the toilet with his glasses broken. So Gunther had had to leave *that* school and had been reassigned a place at Bracket Wood. To which school Frank had grumblingly accepted his son would have to go.

But every day, on the way there, he would warn his son that nothing that Gunther learned at school should be believed. This was because, he explained, most of the 'lessons' – he would do the inverted commas round that word as well; he used the inverted commas mime a *lot* – were, in fact, lies made up by THEM to promote their dark, world-controlling ways.

'What's the latest lie I should watch out for, Dad?' said Gunther, as they walked along the road towards Bracket Wood on the day that the Flackles' relevance to this story became clear (or at least it will in a minute).

'Well, one thing we haven't really properly discussed, son, is . . .' Frank stopped, looked around, as if THEY might be listening – which, of course, THEY were because THEY had cameras and bugs everywhere . . . probably – and then whispered: '*Aliens*.'

'Pardon?' said Gunther.

'Oh, sorry,' said his dad, crouching down – with some difficulty, as he was not a small man – and putting his mouth to his son's ear. '*Aliens*.'

'Oh . . .' said Gunther. 'Yeah.' And then, trying to reproduce the heavy, dramatic, *I-know-something-no-one-else-does* way that his father said the word, he whispered: '*Aliens*.'

Frank got out of his crouching position (again with difficulty) and continued walking towards the school.

'Because,' he said, 'they're all around us. Oh yes. They're not just up there, in the sky. Lots of them are here, disguised as humans. And maybe even as animals!'

'Really?' said Gunther, wide-eyed.

'Thousands.'

As Frank said this, Gunther noticed, walking on the other side of the street, a boy who he'd seen at school already and didn't much like. He was known for inventing things. Gunther didn't like that because it meant the boy was clever, and Gunther didn't like people who were clever. Or at least *thought* they were clever. But they never knew things like his dad did.

Gunther also noticed that the boy was walking with a girl who he *hadn't* seen before. There was something a bit odd about her. Her hair was cut in a strange way, and she was pointing at trees and houses like she'd never seen such things before.

He looked back at his dad. 'How do we spot them?'

Frank nodded, sniffed, gazed all around and put

one finger on one side of his nose then the other.

'Keep 'em peeled,' he said.

Gunther nodded. Then frowned. 'What, my nostrils?'

'No! Your eyes. My finger is touching my nose, yes, but it's pointing up. At my eyes.'

Gunther nodded. Then frowned.

'How do you peel your eyes? Sounds painful.'

'Oh, for crying out loud, Gunther! Just look out for anything . . . strange. Now get off to –' he looked disdainfully at the Bracket Wood gates and raised his fingers for the mime – '"school".'

CHAPTER 16
Bobbins

'Okay, so remember what I told you,' said Rahul.

'This is amazing!' said Pip, looking around and pointing at everything, as she had done all the way to Bracket Wood School. 'I've never been outside for this long before!'

'Yes, anyway, remember, our plan – so you're— '

She threw her head up. 'The sky! It's so *blue*! What are those white things floating through it?'

'Er . . . clouds?

'Wow. We don't have them.'

'You don't?' This sounded, to Rahul, quite worrying. What had happened to *clouds* in the future? He opened his mouth to ask, but Pip was still staring at everything.

'And your houses – they're so *small*! Where are the ones that go up and up and up . . . ?'

'Well, there are some like that in another part of the city . . .'

'And people can just walk about? From place to place?'

'Yes. Like we're doing now.'

'Hey!' said Pip, looking down at her feet. 'I could finally get to use my GravityLess Boots! I could *really* fly!'

She blinked and started to rise into the air. And then sank back to the ground because Rahul had placed his hands on her shoulders.

'Pip!' he said. 'We're trying to keep the fact that

you're from the future secret! I think FLYING in the middle of the street on the way to my school is a bit of a giveaway!'

'Oh. Yes. Sorry.' She blinked, to switch off the boots. 'I really would like to have a proper go with them while I'm here, though . . .'

'I'm sure we'll find a moment. Anyway. The plan is—'

'Oh! No! I'm not having *that*!' cried Pip, and ran over to a woman on the other side of the street.

'Hello? Pip? What are you . . . ?' Rahul ran after her.

The woman, who was quite old, had a small sausage dog on a lead. Pip bent down and picked up the dog.

'I'm sorry!' she said to the woman. 'But you can't do that! Can she?'

'I beg your pardon, young lady?' said the woman.

Pip looked at the sausage dog. The dog was

gazing back at her blankly. Pip read the tag on its collar.

'Bobbins!' she said. 'Is that really your name? Okay, Bobbins,' she said, turning him round to face his owner. 'Explain to this person what it feels like having a leather rope tied round your neck!'

The dog stared at its owner. It whimpered.

'No, no,' said Pip. 'Use your words!'

The dog barked. It wriggled.

'I think what Bobbins is saying, Pip,' said Rahul, 'is *put me down, please. I don't mind the lead.*'

Pip turned the dog to face her. 'Really?'

'Pip,' whispered Rahul. 'They can't speak yet. Remember?'

'Oh yes!' She looked at the very confused old lady. And handed her the dog. 'Sorry!'

CHAPTER 17
Pippa von Vandersteiner

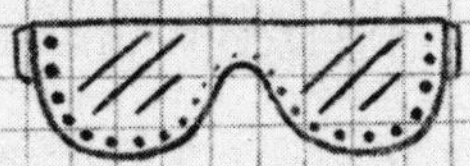

Once they got into the playground, Rahul went over the plan again.

'Okay. So. Where are you from?'

'3020!' said Pip.

'No!' said Rahul. 'In our plan. That we worked out.'

'Oh yes, sorry. What's it called again? Germy?'

'Germany. The country's called Germany.'

'Yes, that's right. We don't have countries any

more in our time. Sorry, it's all very confusing. Plus, I'm a bit tired.'

Which was fair enough. Once Prisha and Sanjay had gone to bed, Rahul had quietly led Pip and Dag back to the warehouse, and tried to make up somewhere for her to sleep. They'd managed to find a camp bed, but the springs had gone long ago, and Pip kept falling through it.

Eventually, they made a bed out of beanbags, with curtains for blankets. At which point, Dag said: 'What about me?' And – as Pip had explained blearily to Rahul the next morning – he carried on complaining all night about the fact that he hadn't got a bed (which he did in his BirdCube at home, a tiny one that he actually lay down on).

In the morning, Rahul saved some toast from his breakfast and brought it across to the warehouse to give to Pip and Dag. Pip loved it, saying that the bread tasted much nicer than any she'd ever had.

They'd left Dag – who said he preferred seeds, thank you – in the warehouse, with strict instructions not to speak (at least no more than *Pretty Polly!*) to anyone who came in.

The plan for the day was as follows: at school, Pip was going to pretend to be Rahul's German exchange. This may seem a strange plan, as Bracket Wood didn't run exchanges with schools in other countries, but Rahul was going to tell them that his mum had organised it all herself because she wanted Rahul to be an expert in languages. This, he knew, would work, as all the staff at Bracket Wood were frightened of Prisha.

'Okay,' said Rahul, just as they were about to go into the school building, 'so, if anyone asks you, you say—'

'OY! Roool!' said a loud voice behind them. 'Or whatever your name is . . .'

Rahul looked round. It was Gunther.

'It's pronounced Rahul.'

'Roool.'

'*Ra*-hul.'

Gunther screwed up his face and pursed his lips, as if warming up in preparation for the immense difficulty of saying it.

'ROOOOL!'

Rahul wiped a fleck of Gunther's spit off his cheek. 'Okay, it'll have to do. What do you want?'

Gunther looked over at Pip suspiciously. 'Who's your friend? I saw her trying to talk to that dog. Bit weird. Bit . . . strange, I reckon.'

Rahul glanced at Pip. 'Um . . . I dunno about that, Gunther. Lots of people talk to animals.'

'Hmm. Not like she did they don't.'

Pip stared at him. She stuck her hand out. 'Hello! My name is Pippa von Vandersteiner. I am from Munich! What is your name?'

Gunther looked at her, but didn't take her hand.

Instead, he tapped both sides of his nose with one finger.

'I'm keeping 'em peeled,' he said and walked away.

Rahul looked at Pip. Pip looked back at him.

'What?' asked Pip. 'His nostrils?'

CHAPTER 18

Don't groan!

The first class was maths with Mr Barrington. Rahul went up to the teacher's desk before the lesson started to introduce him to Pippa von Vandersteiner.

'Oh!' said Mr Barrington, squinting at her through his enormously thick glasses. 'Does the head teacher know about this German boy?'

'Girl,' said Rahul.

'Where I come from girls and boys don't look

that different,' said Pip.

'And also this particular very short-sighted teacher wouldn't have been able to make out which one you were anyway,' said Rahul quietly.

'What was that, Rahul?'

'Nothing, sir. Anyway, I believe the school has been informed about everything to do with Pippa by my mother.'

Mr Barrington looked worried. 'Your mother? The one I met at parents' evening?'

'Who told you *exactly* what standard of teaching she expects from you? Yes, Mr Barrington. That one. I don't have another mum.'

'Hmm. Yes, I remember.' He went a little white. 'Okay, okay, fine. *Guten Morgen*, Pippa. Sit next to Rahul.'

Pip walked back to Rahul's desk and took the chair beside him.

'What did he say just then?' she whispered.

'I think it was "good morning" in German,' said Rahul. 'Hmm. I hadn't thought any of the teachers might actually *speak* German – not at Bracket Wood . . .'

Pippa nodded and then grimaced.

'Are you okay?' said Rahul.

'I don't know,' she replied. 'My stomach kind of hurts . . .'

'Right!' said Mr Barrington. 'Today we're going to be doing . . . prime numbers! Does everyone remember what those are?'

A huge groan went up from the entire class. Sam Green, Barry Bennett, Malcolm Bailey, Ellie and Fred Stone, and Ryan Ward and his friend Dionna all joined in. A girl called Janet, who had a tendency just to say the first thing that came into her head, said: 'Are they a bit like prime ministers?'

'Don't groan!' said Mr Barrington. 'And, Janet: no,

they're not.' He picked up a marker and wrote on the board:

2, 3, 5, 7, 11, 13, 17, 19 . . .

'Right! Can anyone tell me what the next number is in this sequence?'

No one put their hand up.

'Come on! I taught you about prime numbers last week!'

Still no one put their hand up.

'Right. Well. We are all staying here, throughout break, until someone comes up here and writes down the next number in this sequence . . . !' said Mr Barrington, his face turning red.

Pip put her hand up.

'I said, we are all staying here, throughout break, until—'

'Mr Barrington, I have my hand up!' said Pip.

'What? Who said that?'

'Me! Pip. I mean Pippa. Von Vandersteiner.'

'Oh! The German boy!'

'Girl. Yes.'

'Right. Well. Of course, I didn't teach *you* about prime numbers last week. But nonetheless, if you know how the sequence works, come here!'

Pip got up. Rahul touched her arm. 'Are you sure . . . ?'

Pip nodded at him. 'I can do it . . .' And carried on walking.

'That wasn't what I meant,' said Rahul to himself.

'Okay!' said Mr Barrington when she got to him. 'Here's the marker. *Danke schön.*'

'Pardon?' said Pip.

'*Danke schön*. Sorry, I know my accent isn't great . . .'

'Oh. Yes,' said Pip. She turned to the whiteboard, and put on her glasses. She looked at the sum. An eagle-eyed person – which would not, as we know, have included Mr Barrington – might have noticed a tiny flickering of lights round the edge of her glasses frame as she did so.

'Right . . . so if one evaluates the logarithmic integral one over log t with respect to t from zero to x, then that gives us a good first approximation of the number of primes up to x, once, of course, I've applied the Mobius inversion formula, but then I need to introduce the error terms, which correspond to an infinite sum over the zeros of the zeta function where I evaluate the approximation at x to the power of rho for each zero of the zeta function rho.'

She wrote all this out on the board, at super-quick speed. Then she turned to Mr Barrington, to hand him back the marker.

He squinted at her. Then at the whiteboard.

'I beg your pardon?'

'What?'

'I . . . sorry . . . I . . . what's the answer?'

'To what?'

'The question.'

'Pi of x is R of x plus the infinite sum over rho, the zeros of the zeta function, of R of x to the rho.'

Mr Barrington went very red. 'I don't understand.'

'Oh,' said Pip.

'What's the *next number*?' said Mr Barrington.

'Well, obviously, in this particular case, twenty-three . . .'

'Right. Um. Yes. I mean just the number would have been fine.'

'. . . but my equation will work for any x—'

'Yes, yes. Well done. Thank you. Clearly, German primary schools are quite advanced in their maths. *Danke. Geh jetzt zurück zu deinem Platz.*'

Pip smiled blankly.

'*Ja*, Pippa?' said Mr Barrington. '*Geh jetzt zurück zu deinem Platz*?

Pip looked round at Rahul, confused. Rahul was mouthing the words, *'It's German. Say something! Anything!'*

But before that message could get through to Pip, who was staring at him, even more confused, a voice at the back said: 'Mr Barrington?'

'Who said that?'

'Me. Gunther.'

Everyone looked round. Gunther was sitting at his desk with his hand up and a weird smirk on his face.

'Ah,' said Mr Barrington, his heart sinking. An interruption in class from Gunther was never good news. 'Please don't start telling me that this sum is wrong because . . . because the secret lizard overlords are controlling our . . . arithmetic. Or whatever.'

'No, Mr Barrington. I just wondered what language that was that you were just speaking.'

'Oh! German.' He turned to Pip. 'As Pippa can tell you. I picked up a little when I was over there on military service just after the war.'

Rahul frowned: just how old *was* Mr Barrington? But, before he could think that through, Gunther said: 'Can she?'

'Pardon?'

'Can "Pippa" tell us? She doesn't seem to have understood a word you've said.'

'Well,' said Mr Barrington, 'I don't know why you've done that inverted commas mime over the word *Pippa*. But I'm sure that isn't true.'

'Er . . .' said Pip.

'However, that's not a bad idea in a way, Gunther. It's a maths class, but why not do a tiny bit of languages, eh? So, Pippa. Please reply to my questions in your native tongue. *Wie geht es dir heute*?'

Which means *How are you today*? in German.

But Pip didn't know that. She looked at Rahul in confusion.

And Gunther's smirk widened.

CHAPTER 19
WIE GEHT ES DIR HEUTE?

'Pippa?' said Mr Barrington. '*Wie geht es dir heute*?'

'Um . . .' said Pip. 'Can you say that just one more time?'

'Sorry? Can you not hear me?'

'Er . . . no. I'm a bit deaf. It helps if you look at me while you say it.'

'Oh. Right. You're lip-reading?'

'Kind of.'

'Right. Well, either you are or you aren't, Pippa.'

'Mr Barrington,' said Gunther. 'I think she's . . . stalling. Why would she be doing that? Unless she *isn't* really German?' He looked round at the rest of the class. '*Hmmmmmm . . . ?*'

They looked back at him, baffled. They were used, by now, to Gunther's weird ideas. But what this had to do with the new German girl no one could work out.

Mr Barrington stared at him in confusion too.

'What are you on about, Gunther? Why would she say she was German if she was from another part of the world?'

'Aha!' said Gunther. 'Maybe she's *not* from another part of the world! Not *this* world anyway!'

Mr Barrington frowned. 'What? You're saying that Pippa von Vandersteiner is an—'

'I'm not stalling!' said Pip. 'I just need . . .' She reached up, got hold of Mr Barrington's chin and pulled his face towards her.

'Ugh! Please don't touch my chin!'

'Sorry!'

'Or any other part of me!'

'Sorry! We Germans are very . . . tactile. But I do need to see your face when you ask me the question.'

He leaned his face very close to her. 'Pippa! *WIE GEHT ES DIR HEUTE?*'

'Ah,' said Pip. 'Thank you. That's perfect.' The lights on her glasses flickered briefly, and then she turned to the class and said, in a perfect German accent:

'Mir geht es super, danke Ihnen, und es ist toll, hier zu sein, in diesem sehr schönen Klassenzimmer, und an Ihrem Unterricht teilzunehmen, Herr Barrington.'

Which means: *I am great, thank you, and it's amazing to be here in your lovely classroom, taking part in your lessons, Mr Barrington.*

It went on quite a lot longer, this speech in German. (I won't put it all in because this is a children's book, and I can't expect non-German children reading it to understand another language. Actually, my books are translated into German, and I frankly have no idea how they're going to do this bit. I'll leave that to them.)

Pip spoke for some time about Bracket Wood and how much she was looking forward to being there. In German. Which left no one listening in any doubt that Pippa von Vandersteiner was indeed German.

Apart from Rahul.

When she'd finished and gone back to her seat, he whispered: 'How did you do *that*? How did you even know what he was saying?'

She whispered back: 'My G-Glasses translated it. They just needed to *see* as well as *hear* what he was saying. Although, even then, it took a while for them to find the language. German doesn't exist in 3020. My Translate Box only had it down as an ancient, dead tongue.'

'Like Latin?'

'Is that an old language now?'

'Yes.'

'So, anyway, the glasses then gave me the translation of what I wanted to say back . . . and I just read it out!'

'But how did you manage to sound so *German*?'

'Oh, the Translate Box links up with the part of my brain that controls my voice and makes sure I pronounce every word correctly. I have no idea, obviously, what Germs sound like.'

'Germans.'

'Germans, right.'

A scrunched-up bit of paper hit Rahul on the side of the head. 'Ow!' he said and looked over.

When I said earlier that the speech in German left no one in the classroom in any doubt that Pippa von Vandersteiner was indeed German – apart from Rahul – that wasn't quite true. There was another person who remained unconvinced. Perhaps you can guess who that was.

'Can you please not throw paper at me, Gunther?' said Rahul, looking behind him.

Gunther just stared at him. And Pip.

'I dunno how you did that, "Pippa" . . .'

'Please stop doing that inverted commas mime,' said Rahul.

'. . . but, then again, I have no idea what you people . . . I say people –' he started to do the inverted commas mime around *people*, but then thought better of it – 'anyway . . . *what* you can do. But I know this.'

Once again, he placed his finger either side of his nose.

'Keeping 'em peeled, Rool. Keeping. 'Em. Peeled.'

He looked away at that point, out of

the window, clearly thinking: *That's a mic drop. That's an exit line. That's them told. Game* over.

Unfortunately for him, Rahul then said: '*Rahul.*'

'What?' said Gunther, trying not to look back at him, trying not to ruin the moment.

'My name is Rahul.'

'Yeah. Whatever,' muttered Gunther, annoyed.

CHAPTER 20

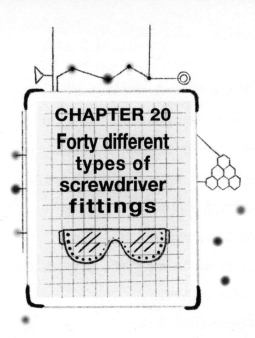

Forty different types of screwdriver fittings

'How's your stomach ache?' said Rahul, as they were walking back to his flat.

'Still hurts a bit,' said Pip. 'I think it could be the food here. I like it – that bread you brought me this morning was so tasty – but my stomach might not be used to it.'

As she said this, they reached the warehouse doors and Rahul held up a hand. They hesitated before entering. Someone was in there, talking.

'Who is it?' asked Pip.

'I think it's my dad . . .' said Rahul.

He opened the door and looked in. Sanjay was bending over Dag, who was perched on top of a crate full of cans of mini sausages and beans. Sanjay was holding some seeds in his palm.

'Come on, parrot. Come on, mate. I know you can say more than that.'

'Pretty Polly! Pretty Polly!' said Dag.

'Yes. I got that. But look. Seeds! If you say something else.'

'Pretty Polly!'

'Just one other thing!'

'PRETTY POLLY!'

'Hmm,' said Rahul. 'I'd better go and rescue Dag. You'd best switch your suit to *Invisible*.'

'Okay,' said Pip and blinked twice. Nothing happened. She started going into the warehouse.

'Er . . .' said Rahul. 'It hasn't worked.'

'What?'

'I can see you.'

'Oh!' said Pip.

'Can't you tell? Shouldn't you . . . not be able to see your hands?'

'No!' she replied. 'I can always see myself. It's only other people who can't. It deflects the light from *outside*.'

'So . . .'

'So, clearly, it's running out of power. Let me give it another go.'

'No, no. If it's running out of power, we need to save it. For school. And whatever else. I'll just tell my dad you're a new friend from school – he never knows who my friends are. That's just a thing with dads.'

'Is it?' said Pip.

'Well,' said Rahul, 'yeah. Isn't it in your time?'

'I don't really have any friends. I do know some

people my age who are on the Grid. They're in the same Learning Matrix as me. But I've never met them in . . .' She frowned, searching for the word.

'Real life?' said Rahul.

Pip laughed. 'Yes. I guess. We don't use that expression in 3020 – we think how we live, mainly online, *is* real life – but yes.'

'Rahul?' called Sanjay. 'Is that you?'

'Er . . . yes, Dad!' he said. He went into the warehouse.

Pip looked nervous.

'Hey,' said Rahul. 'It'll be okay.'

Pip nodded and they walked in.

'Hi, Dad!' said Rahul. 'This is my friend Pip, from school.'

'Oh, hello,' said Sanjay, hardly noticing her.

Rahul did a *you see*? face at Pip.

'This parrot. I'm sure it was able to say more things when it first appeared. Now all it says is—'

'PRETTY POLLY!' said Dag. He was screaming it, very loudly, at Rahul and Pip. 'PRETTY. PRETTY. POLLY!'

'It's almost like he's angry about it,' said Sanjay. 'Like, furious . . . like he wants to *swear* or something in between the words Pretty and Polly . . .'

'Yes. Anyway, Dad, Mum wanted to speak to you?'

'She did?' said Sanjay, looking worried. 'Okay.' And he rushed out.

Pip and Rahul looked at Dag. Dag opened his wings, shook his head and screamed:

'OMG! I HAVE HAD TO SIT HERE AND JUST SQUAWK PRETTY BLO—'

'Don't swear, Dag,' said Pip.

'. . . GRRR . . . POLLY ALL DAY! YOUR DAD HAS BEEN HANGING ON TO THOSE SEEDS, TRYING TO GET ME TO SAY SOMETHING CLEVER, AND BECAUSE YOU SAID I COULDN'T HE'S HARDLY GIVEN ME ANY AND NOW I'M STARVING!'

'Sorry, Dag!' said Rahul, opening a new box of seeds from an enormous sack.

'I WAS ON THE VERGE OF JUST SAYING, "LISTEN, SANJAY. I'M FROM THE FUTURE. I CAN SPEAK, I WOULD SAY, CONSIDERABLY BETTER THAN MOST HUMANS I'VE MET HERE. ALSO, YOU SEEM TO BE FRIGHTENED OF YOUR WIFE."'

'Please don't say any of that, Dag,' said Rahul, offering him some seeds in his palm.

Dag tucked in.

'*Num num num* . . . I must say these are very good . . . obviously, in 3020, the seeds are grown in laboratories . . . they don't have this . . . authentic flavour . . .'

'Perhaps Dag's Channel Five show should be a cookery one?' said Pip.

Rahul laughed. 'You're getting the hang of living in this time now, aren't you?'

'I like it. It's fun!' said Pip. She rubbed her tummy.

'But there is the stomach ache. We didn't even have lunch at school today because of it. So I'd like to know that we could get back to my family at some point!'

Rahul looked over at the toilet seat from which Pip and Dag had emerged yesterday. The lid remained firmly shut. He picked up a yellow box from a shelf behind him and opened it.

'What's that?' said Pip.

'A toolkit.'

Pip came over and peered inside. 'What are those?'

'Forty different types of screwdriver fitting. And a wrench.'

'Right. None of those were words I understood.'

'I'm not sure how any of this is going to help.' Rahul shut the toolkit.

Pip looked at him. 'Come on, Rahul. I can tell already – even though we've only just met, and I've not really even met anyone before – that you're someone who doesn't think in straight lines. You think differently from most people. *That's* what you need to do here . . .'

Rahul nodded and stood a little taller. 'Okay,' he said. 'I'll try.'

CHAPTER 21

Tweet, tweet tweet tweet tweet

Rahul crouched down and examined the toilet seat. He tried to lift the lid again, but it was stuck fast.

'So,' he said. 'First principles. This is a toilet seat. Therefore it should be positioned like it would be . . . on a toilet!'

'Right,' said Pip. 'I'm not sure that really *is* thinking outside the box exactly.'

'No, but we've been assuming that the portal

comes through the wall of the warehouse. It doesn't, does it? It operates through time not space.'

'How do you mean?'

'I think this – where we are now – is where you live. In 3020. I think it's the same spot.'

Pip looked around. 'Maybe . . .'

'So,' said Rahul, 'let's move the toilet seat away from the wall – it doesn't need to be there – and lay it flat on the ground.'

'Ha ha ha ha ha!' said Dag.

'What's so funny?' said Pip.

'It looks like there's an enormous toilet underneath that.'

'Good one,' said Rahul. 'So I have an idea.' He went back to the toolkit and got out a wrench and a hammer. Then he went to the toilet seat, placed the wrench in the gap between the lid and the seat, and started to hammer at it. *BANG! BANG!*

'Um . . .' said Pip, 'I'm a bit worried you're going to break it . . . ?'

'No, it's okay. This wrench is too thin to break anything. I just want to wedge it in between . . .' *BANG!* '. . . the lid and the seat . . .' *BANG! BANG!*

It worked. Each tap of the hammer pushed the wrench further between the toilet lid and the seat, until the whole thing disappeared, except for two bits sticking out at either end.

'Right. Good,' said Rahul. 'Now, Pip, can you get hold of the far end? And I'll try this one.'

Pip put her hand round one end of the wrench. Rahul put his round the other.

'Okay! Push up!'

She did and he did. Which meant that, together, they lifted the toilet seat up in the air, above their heads.

'Great!' said Dag. 'You look like a sports team that have just won the Toilet Seat Trophy!'

'I'm really starting to wonder how humanity made it to 3020,' said Pip, looking at Rahul.

When they put it down again, though, the lid was open!

'Aha!' said Rahul. 'It must have been the gravitational power of us pulling the seat upwards that acted against the mass of the lid, forcing it open!'

'Yes,' said Pip. 'Or it just opened because it wasn't *that* stuck.'

'Well. Yes,' said Rahul. He peered into it. 'I can't see anything. Just the floor,' he said.

Pip had a look as well. 'We have to get them to open the portal from their side too.'

'Hmm. Is there a very . . . you know . . . year 3020, state-of-the-art, hi-tech way of doing that?'

Pip bent her head back down over the toilet seat. 'Mum! Dad! It's Pip! HELLO!'

'Right,' said Rahul. 'I see.'

'Let me have a go,' said Dag, perching on the seat and looking in.

'Are you just going to shout hello as well?'

'Don't be stupid,' he said. And then he started singing. But not, as you might expect, some complicated song with words. No: what he sang was birdsong.

Tweet tweet tweet tweet tweet . . .

'Wow,' said Rahul. 'I didn't realise you could still speak . . . parrot?'

'Of course I can,' said Dag. '*Tweet tweet tweet . . .*'

'I mean, great . . . but why?'

'It's a different frequency,' said Pip. 'It travels quicker and further through the portal.'

Dag continued to sing. They all looked into the blackness. Rahul found himself thinking: *How did I get here? Watching a parrot sing into a toilet*?

But suddenly a circle of light appeared in the oval of the toilet seat. And then a face!

Of a cat.

CHAPTER 22
Meow

'Hello, Dag,' called Squeezy-Paws across the centuries. 'Hello, Pip. How's things?'

'Well. Not quite how I expected, to be honest,' called back Pip. 'We're not at the Stadium Above the Clouds. We're in 2019!'

Squeezy-Paws nodded. 'Oops.'

'Yeah. Oops indeed. Can you get Mum and Dad? To open the portal on your side?'

'Um . . .' said Squeezy-Paws. 'Not sure.'

'Pardon?'

'Well . . .'

Suddenly the cat's face was gone, replaced by what, to Rahul, looked like a mirror with the reflection looking back at Pip.

Only then the reflection started talking. 'Hello, Pip. Mum and Dad aren't in.'

'Eh? They're always in.'

'Sorry. I'll pass on your message. Bye!'

After that, a dark shadow began to steal over the oval of light, as if a door was being shut at that end of the portal.

'What? No!' said Pip. 'Pip 2! Go and get them *now*!'

'Um . . .' said Rahul. 'What's going on?'

'It's Pip's RoboClone,' said Dag.

'Oh,' said Rahul. 'Of course. I won't even ask about the talking cat.'

Suddenly Squeezy-Paws's face appeared again, in

a little corner of light still left in the oval. As if she had squeezed in between the door and the edge of the portal, stopping it from shutting. She spoke very quickly.

'Okay, so Pip 2 has gone a bit mad – it's convinced your mum and dad that it *is* you and, to be honest, it is very good at being you, maybe even better at being you than you are. Anyway, it shut the portal and *owwww*!'

Pip 2's hand appeared, grabbing hold of Squeezy-Paws's head.

'Ow! Get off! Ow! Pip! I tried to tell them, but it threatened to send me down here as well and . . .'

Seconds later, a voice shouted: 'NOT IT! SHE!' and Squeezy-Paws's little head suddenly got larger. And larger. Then *much* larger.

Until eventually it popped out of the toilet seat in 2019.

'Meow,' said Squeezy-Paws ironically.

CHAPTER 23

MindLink

‘I tell you one thing about this . . . RoboClone,’ said Rahul, after Pip had made sure that her cat had no serious injuries. ‘It’s strong. That cat came flying down the portal! And he’s an absolute unit!’

‘Excuse me,’ said Squeezy-Paws. ‘I can understand you, remember? Also, I am a she. Obviously. I am a very elegant, comfortable-in-my-size, furry lady.’

‘Oh yes. Sorry.’ Rahul turned to Pip. ‘What’s the deal with the clone?’

Pip took a deep breath. 'My mum and dad bought it for me a few years ago. As a kind of playmate because I don't get to meet any other children. I really loved it at first. But as we grew up—'

'Sorry, a robot can grow . . . ?'

'Yes. Is that weird?'

Rahul shook his head. 'Maybe no weirder than that furry chonk popping out of the toilet seat just now.'

'EXCUSE ME!' said Squeezy-Paws. 'AGAIN!'

'Sorry.'

'We grew apart,' continued Pip sadly. 'And . . . I guess . . . it – um, *she* – must have had MindLink on, without me realising. Or just overheard maybe.'

'What?'

'My parents were talking about getting a new RoboClone. Well, *Dag* was talking about them talking about it. To me. It might have hurt its – her – feelings. I feel bad now.'

'Can robots have feelings?'

'Yes. About a hundred years ago – well, nine hundred years from now – scientists created robots that had human emotions. Humans who liked hanging out with robots wanted that. But . . .'

'Yes?' said Rahul.

'Well, they're not meant to have *bad* emotions. Y'know, jealousy, envy, anger. Trying to take someone else's place. But maybe that's changed . . .'

Rahul got out his notebook and wrote that down. 'This is all so interesting,' he said.

'Interesting. But not good.' She shook her head. 'But I can't believe that my parents really can't tell the difference between me and Pip 2!'

Squeezy-Paws looked up at her. 'She is a pretty exact match.'

'That's the weird thing about clones, eh, cat?' said Dag, fluttering down next to her.

'Oh yeah. Of course. *You're* here.'

'Another remarkable piece of cat perception. No

wonder humans think you're more intelligent than dogs.'

'Well, we are.'

'Actually, that's true,' said Pip to Rahul. 'The dogs never say anything more than, "This is great! Really great! I love everything!"' She turned back to Dag and Squeezy-Paws. 'But we've got more important things to think about. Like how to get back home. So I'd prefer you two not to argue about everything as usual.'

Dag and Squeezy-Paws looked at each other as if to say: *Hmmm – we'll see about that.*

'You mentioned that Pip 2 maybe overheard what Dag said – or maybe had MindLink on. What does that mean?' asked Rahul.

Pip tapped her head. 'We can link our minds. Anyone can in 3020. That was fun at first too – we could share funny pictures. Or whatever.'

'So if Pip 2 is a robot with cameras of some

kind for eyes . . . and everything in 3020 happens online . . . and you have that MindLink –' Rahul tapped his finger on his forehead as if he had one implanted there too (he didn't) – 'could you see what Pip 2 sees? Remotely?'

Pip stared at him. 'Yes! You're right. I can access her point of view, like a camera.'

'And . . . would she know?'

'No. I don't think so. You can customise the privacy settings, but we never bothered.'

'Well, it might be useful to MindLink now then,' said Rahul. 'So we can find out what's going on.'

'Okay. But that's when we're in the same HouseUnit. And . . . y'know . . . century.'

'Yep. But we have a portal here. And, even though the lid's closed, I would've thought Wi-Fi or Bluetooth or whatever the electromagnetic waves that transmit information are called in *your* time will work through it?'

Pip thought about this.

'I agree,' said Dag.

'So do I,' said Squeezy-Paws.

'Oh, like *you* know anything about it.'

'Well, I think *I'm* the one who was just *in* 3020!'

'Yes and got thrown down the portal like a furry medicine ball!'

'He's right!' said Pip.

'Please don't say that!' said Squeezy-Paws. 'I'm trying to diet!'

'No! Rahul! He's right!'

Everyone turned round. Pip had her eyes shut.

'I've used my MindLink to access Pip 2's POV.' She turned to them, keeping her eyes closed. 'I can see our HouseUnit! I can *see* 3020!'

CHAPTER 24

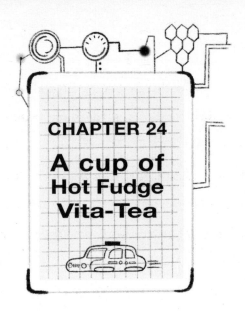

A cup of Hot Fudge Vita-Tea

'Ooh,' said Squeezy-Paws. 'Can we see?'

'Cat. You were just there a *minute* ago!'

'I think you'll find, parrot, that it was a thousand and one years ago.'

'No, I think *you'll* find it was a thousand and one years in the future. *This* is a thousand and one years ago.'

'Actually,' said Rahul, '*can* we see? *Can* you project what you're seeing on to another screen? I'd love to be able to look at your world . . .'

'Um . . .' said Pip. 'I guess. Probably easier to use my G-Glasses.' She put them on. 'Have you got another screen?'

'So ahead of you!' said Rahul.

While Pip's eyes had been closed, and the animals were having another argument, he'd got up and found, in the electronics section of the warehouse, a laptop computer. It had been made in 2013, and was about four times as thick as laptops are now – at least in 2019 – plus, someone had written on it, in white marker, DO NOT RESELL – but, when Rahul opened it, it went *DING!*

He sat cross-legged on the floor with the computer next to him. Dag flew on to his lap, and Squeezy-Paws stood by his knee.

'Pip. Can you see this computer in your –' Rahul searched for the phrase – 'I want to say on-head Wi-Fi?'

The lights flickered round the edges of her G-Glasses.

'Something's come up,' said Pip. 'Er . . . DAPPLE?'

'That's it.'

'It's actually called DAPPLE?'

'Yes. That's the make of the computer.'

'If I remember my twenty-first-century history, there was another company called something very—'

'Yes, never mind. Can you sync with it?'

She nodded. Seconds later, an image came up on Rahul's DAPPLE screen. He peered at it.

'I can't believe it. This really is a thousand years from now!'

On the screen was what looked like a very bare flat. Everything was white. There were no pictures on the walls. There was a large main room. In the middle of it was a see-through box suspended from the ceiling in which Rahul could just make out a tiny bed.

'That's my BirdCube!' said Dag.

'Amazing,' said Rahul.

'So comfy! But also very small.'

'Where's the spaceships? And the laser guns that take a quick X-ray of their victims before they kill them?'

'Don't believe everything you see in your science-fiction films, Rahul,' said Pip.

The image swerved, as if a camera was moving about. On the screen, there was what looked like a porthole off to one side of the room.

'That's where the LabSpace is,' said Pip. She'd taken off her G-Glasses and come to join them, kneeling down next to Rahul. 'Behind that window. I see they've cleaned it up . . .'

The image moved again. There was a longer window running down one side of the room.

'What is that?' said Rahul.

'Outside,' said Pip.

Rahul gulped. 'Why is it that colour?'

'It's the sky. I told you. In 3020, it's red.'

'Hmm. That's a bit frightening.'

'Yes,' said Pip. 'And, like I said, it's really hot, and there's loads of floods, and viruses . . . that's why we can't go outside. It is frightening in my world.'

'Can't anything be done about that?' said Rahul.

'That's what my parents have been trying to do.' She turned to him. 'But, when I say *my* world, of course it's the *same* world as this one. So, I think that whatever went wrong . . . probably started round about now.'

Rahul nodded. She was right. He had just started to think about how things could perhaps turn out differently when a voice on the screen said: 'Hey! Pip!'

The image on the laptop shifted quickly to the right to reveal a white chair. Which might not have been very interesting except the chair was floating a metre or so in the air. Sitting on it was a woman.

She had black hair, and a kind, if tired, face.

'Mum!' said Pip (the one in 2019). 'Oh! Mum!' She turned to Rahul. 'Okay. I'm sure she'll be able to tell the RoboClone isn't me . . .'

'Is that for me?' said Pip's mum to the screen. The screen nodded and a hand, coming from behind the camera, held out a cup. The woman pressed a button on the arm of the chair. It floated, carrying her towards the screen.

'Hot Fudge flavour Vita-Tea!' said Nina. 'My favourite!'

'I know,' said Pip 2's voice. 'And I know you like a cuppa at this time of day . . .'

Nina smiled, holding out a hand. The hand went behind the screen, as if it was rubbing Pip 2's cheek.

'You're such a good daughter. Aren't you?'

Pip – the real one – went red in the face. 'OH! What is that RoboClone doing?'

'It's being nicer than you!' said Dag.

'Dag!' said Squeezy-Paws. 'Be sensitive.'

'It's not being *nicer* than me!' said Pip. 'It's just . . . sucking up to my mum. But my dad – he'll *definitely* have noticed a difference.

I'm sure of it!'

'Hey! Is that a cup of Hot Fudge Vita-Tea?' said a voice, and a man appeared. He was tall and wore large black spectacles, which looked like an adult version of Pip's G-Glasses.

'Is that him?' said Rahul, and Pip nodded.

'Don't worry,' said Pip 2's voice with a chuckle. 'I did one for you too!'

A cup appeared from behind the screen again. Ivan reached for it and took a long drink. While he was doing this, another white chair floated into shot behind him. He sat down in it, still holding the cup.

'That was delicious, Pip, thank you. Do you know what? I was just saying to your mother how nice you've been over the last few days!'

'Yes,' said Nina. 'I thought recently that something was wrong with you. Like that day when I had so much trouble getting you out of bed!'

'You're right,' said Pip 2. 'I wasn't feeling quite myself.'

'Well,' said Ivan, 'in that case, I think you're right

back to being *you*, darling. Lovely, helpful, friendly, best-part-of-the-family Pip!'

And then Pip's dad's face came right up to the screen, lips pursed.

'URRRGHH!' said Dag.

'He does that to me a lot,' said Squeezy-Paws. 'I've told him I don't like it.'

Pip stared at the screen silently.

'Pip?' said Rahul. 'Are you okay?'

She didn't say anything, but shook her head and dropped her gaze.

Rahul gently shut the laptop screen.

'Don't be upset, Pip. It's not their fault,' he said.

Pip nodded. 'I know. But it still feels really weird.'

'Um,' said Rahul, 'where do they think your RoboClone has gone? If they think the real RoboClone is Pip?'

'They probably haven't even noticed that Pip 2's missing. My mum and dad spend most of their time thinking about work, to be honest.'

'And what about us?' said Dag. 'Me and Squeezy-Paws. They didn't even mention us! Especially me! I've been gone for days.'

'Yes,' said Squeezy-Paws. 'But they must notice we've gone soon.'

'Will they?' said Dag.

'Well, definitely,' said Squeezy-Paws. Then she paused. 'Won't they?'

Dag's face fell. 'They don't care about us.'

Squeezy-Paws looked horrified. 'YOU'RE RIGHT! THEY DON'T CARE ABOUT US! THEY DON'T CARE!'

'Calm down, cat. Sanjay and Prisha will hear!'

'Who?'

'Rahul's mum and dad. Who own this warehouse!'

'AT LEAST THAT WOULD BE A MUM AND DAD NOTICING US!' she yowled again.

Rahul looked at Pip, who was still very quiet and

sad. He thought for a minute and then said:

'Tomorrow's a new day, Pip. And I *know* what'll cheer you up!'

CHAPTER 25
IS THAT THE BELL?

'I'm sure of it, Dad. *Sure*,' whispered Gunther.

Frank Flackle stood in the playground at Bracket Wood, next to his son, and looked over at the football match. It was just a playground game, on the little patch of concrete marked out as a pitch in chalk. But one person was dominating it.

'I mean, for a start,' his son continued, 'she's a girl. She shouldn't *be* that good at football.'

Frank raised an eyebrow. The girl Gunther was

referring to – Pippa von Vandersteiner – had just beaten four players and back-heeled the ball into the goal: her eleventh of the game. She ran to high-five with Rahul, who was playing in defence on the same side.

'You were right!' said Pip. 'Football is the answer! I feel so much better now!'

He smiled, gave her a thumbs up and she ran back to the game.

'Hmm . . .' said Frank. 'Well, son, I certainly agree with you that there's something not right about girls playing football. I don't hold with it at all. But that, I'm afraid, is the modern world. That, I'm afraid, is one of the things that THEY have imposed on us. To thwart the natural order.'

Gunther nodded. Then frowned. 'Who are THEY again?'

'Shh,' said his dad. 'Never ask that question out loud.'

'Right. Sorry.'

'But,' said Frank, 'I'm not totally convinced that this girl, strange though she is, is . . . what you say she is.'

Gunther looked up, disappointed. He had thought that his suspicion – that Pippa von Vandersteiner was not Pippa von Vandersteiner, but an alien from another planet – was going to make his dad very, very excited. And very, very pleased with him. He wasn't used to his dad having *doubts*. Well, not about anything that didn't come from THEM anyway.

'She is, Dad! I'm sure she is!' he said, almost in tears.

'Well . . .'

'Oh, forget it!' said Gunther and ran on to the pitch. He was very angry. And, because he was very angry, he ignored the other players saying, 'Hey!' and, 'Which side are you on?' and just made straight for the main object of his fury.

Pip had the ball and had just beaten another three players and was heading again for the goal. Gunther, though, was heading for her. And Gunther was not interested in playing the ball. Pip couldn't see him powering towards her from behind. She was, however, faster than Gunther, who was, like his dad, quite . . . big-boned. Gunther was puffing and panting as Pip raced towards yet another goal. So, in desperation, Gunther just threw himself at her. He put his head down and dived at her like a missile.

It looked as if it was going to be a very painful, very bad tackle. But Rahul shouted: 'PIP! I MEAN . . . PIPPA! WATCH OUT!'

And Pip jumped out of the way. Gunther went sailing past her and hit the ground about a metre further on (he, in fact, went *into* the goal, although since he didn't bring the ball with him it didn't count).

Which would not have been that much of an incident, really, were it not for the fact that Rahul then had to shout: 'PIPPA!'

'What?'

'TURN THEM OFF!'

Pip/Pippa was hovering a metre or so off the ground. In her GravityLess Boots. All the other players were – not unreasonably – staring at her.

'Ah. Yes,' said Pip. She blinked and floated down.

'WOW! PIPPA!' shouted Rahul. 'WHAT AN AMAZING . . . JUMP. IT WAS ALMOST LIKE YOU HOVERED IN THE AIR THERE.'

'No,' said Janet, appearing next to Rahul. 'She *did* hover in the air. For quite a long time.'

'NO!' said Rahul. 'PIPPA'S JUST . . . REALLY GOOD AT JUMPING. IT'S . . . A GERMAN THING. LIKE . . . PENALTIES!'

'YES!' shouted Pippa back. 'LIKE . . . PENALTIES!'

'Can you do it again?' asked Barry Bennett.

'Well, maybe . . .' said Pippa, starting to blink.

'NO!' shouted Rahul. 'OH! IS THAT THE BELL?'

'No,' said Fred Stone.

'YES, IT IS!' Rahul turned away. 'BRRRRRRRRR-RRRRRINGGGGGGGG!'

'That's just you making a bell noise,' said Sam Green.

'WELL, EITHER WAY—'

'Why are you shouting?'

Suddenly a proper bell sound did ring out. Except it didn't seem to be coming from the school. It seemed to be coming from Pippa's uniform. As if it had speakers in it. Or something.

'Well, there we are,' said Rahul, going over to Pip and leading her away from the football pitch. 'Time to get back to class.'

Confused, all the other children watched them go. Except for one. Gunther, despite his quite badly scraped face, was smiling. He was looking at his dad, who was still in the playground and had witnessed the whole thing. Gunther's smile was one that said: *See?*

Frank nodded at him very, very slowly, then touched his finger to both sides of his nose.

CHAPTER 26

And not just pig colds

'Do you think anyone spotted it?' whispered Pip, as they stood, holding trays, in the queue for lunch. Pip and Rahul were still not sure she was able to digest food from 2019, but she had to eat something, so they decided – perhaps bravely – to try what the dinner ladies cooked up at Bracket Wood.

'Do I think anyone spotted you hovering a metre above the ground? For about thirty seconds?' said Rahul. 'Yes. I think just about *everyone*.'

'Oh dear,' said Pip.

'It's a primary school. I don't think anyone will really give it that much thought . . . except for *him*.' Rahul nodded towards Gunther, who was being served in front of them. 'Although, thankfully, right now he's thinking about something else . . .'

'I'll have five scoops of mashed potato,' Gunther was saying, without saying please.

'You're only allowed to have two!' said L'Shaniqua, one of the dinner ladies. 'Isn't that right, Lisa?'

'Two. Maximum,' said her friend.

'That's what you've been told, isn't it? By THEM. Wake up, sheeple!'

Lisa took the scoop from L'Shaniqua's hand and doled out one scoop of mashed potato. Then she nodded at Pip. 'Next!'

Gunther walked away unhappily.

'What is this food?' asked Pip, inspecting the trays in front of her.

Lisa stared at her. 'Sausage and mash. Obviously. It's always sausage and mash on Tuesdays.'

Pip looked confused. 'Sausage . . . ?'

'Pork,' said Rahul.

She still looked confused.

'Pig.'

Her eyes went wide. 'You eat pigs?'

'Well, actually, no, I don't,' said Rahul. 'But yes, people do.'

'But . . . but . . .' Pip turned to the dining hall. 'EVERYBODY! STOP EATING THE – what are they called?'

'Sausages,' said Rahul. 'But—'

'SAUSAGES!'

A few pupils put down their cutlery and looked round.

'You're eating *pigs*! And pigs are so clever! They're cleverer than *us*!'

'Are they?' said Barry Bennett.

'I knew that,' said Janet. 'I've seen *Babe*.'

'She's right,' said Malcolm Bailey. 'Not sure how she knows, though.' He called out to her: 'Have you met Ludwig?'

'A pig will one day invent a cure for the common cold!' said Pip, continuing to address the room. 'And not just pig colds!'

Janet nodded again. 'A pig cold must be quite bad, actually. When you think how big their snouts are,' she said.

'Who *is* that girl?' asked Pip.

'Janet,' said Rahul wearily. 'She's a bit . . . eccentric.'

By now, the whole dining hall was looking at Pip. She drew herself up to her full height.

'YOU'RE EATING THE GREAT-GRANDFATHERS AND GREAT-GRANDMOTHERS OF FUTURE NOBEL PRIZEWINNERS!' she shouted.

There was a short pause after this. Everyone

looked very confused. Then Rahul screwed up his face apologetically and said: 'Vegan. They're really very committed to it in Germany.'

Before quickly leading Pip away.

CHAPTER 27

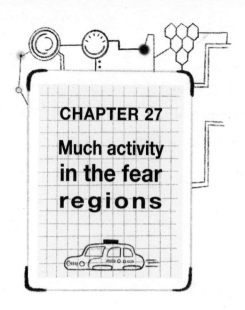

Much activity in the fear regions

'Pip,' said Rahul when they were sitting down, 'you really have to be more careful about drawing attention to yourself.' He looked over his shoulder. 'Gunther's staring at you,' he whispered.

'Hmm. Yes. Right,' she said. 'But just let me enjoy my lunch.' Rahul looked at her plate. It only had two scoops of mash on it. 'I've never tried anything like this!'

'It's school mashed potato.'

'I've never tasted real potato!'

'It isn't real potato. They make it from a packet. Which, in the old days, alien robots used to advertise.'

'Oh. You have alien robots? Even we don't have those!'

Rahul sighed. He liked Pip, but talking to her was sometimes complicated. She forked up more food from her plate. But then frowned and touched her tummy.

'What's wrong?' said Rahul.

'My stomach feels weird again.'

Rahul shook his head. 'Something about our food definitely doesn't agree with you .'

'What was that, Rahill! *Our* food? What do you mean –' asked Gunther, coming over to their table, carrying his empty plates on a tray – 'by that?' He poked Rahul in the chest. 'Eh? Eh? Eh?'

'Nothing really,' said Rahul. 'As in . . . um . . .

British food. As opposed to German!'

'Hmm,' said Gunther. 'Well, if our food's so horrible, you won't mind me taking yours then!'

He picked up Rahul's plate and scraped his lunch on to his own.

'Hey! I hadn't finished that! I was looking forward to my mash!'

'Well, now *I'm* looking forward to your mash,' said Gunther. Then he looked down at his plate. 'Oops! I mean *my* mash.'

Rahul looked around. There didn't seem to be any teachers in the dining hall.

'Oh, sorry, Ruuul,' said Gunther. 'Are you going to cry?'

'No,' said Rahul, although he did look a bit like he might.

'You sure?'

'I'm just hungry . . .'

'That's a shame.'

With that, Gunther raised his fork – actually his spoon because he found eating mash with a fork a bit difficult – and was about to tuck in when a voice said: 'Gunther.'

He looked up, mash halfway to his mouth. 'Oh. It's . . . Okay, I'm doing inverted commas. I mean I'm *not* because I've got a spoonful of mash in my hand, but let's just imagine I am, and you can tell because of the way I'm saying sarcastically . . . *Pippa. Von. Vandersteiner.*'

'Yes. Hello.'

'I noticed during that weird speech about pigs you just gave that you didn't have much of a German accent. Do you . . . oh, hang on a minute.' He put his spoon down and raised his index fingers. '"*Pippa*?"'

Pip nodded and blinked.

'*Ja*. Vell. Zumtimes I do . . . and zumtimes I do not,' she said, sounding very German indeed.

'Hmm.'

'Anyvays, Gunther . . . zat is a German name, *ja*?'

'Um . . . not sure.'

'*Ja*. I zink it is time to give ze potato mash back to the Rahul.'

Gunther nodded. He picked up a spoonful of mash and ate it. Then he stood up and said aggressively, 'And *who* is going to make me do that?'

Pip took out her G-Glasses and put them on. She looked him up and down. There was a faint flickering of light at the sides of her specs.

'Me,' she said.

Gunther laughed.

Pip didn't.

'Zo,' she said. 'You, Gunther, are for sure someone whose brain reveals a large store of anxiety. Der anxiety is created because of a lack of self-esteem. Because you do not truly believe yourself worthy of love.'

'Eh?'

'It – your brain – also stores very much anger. That too is because you don't think you are loved. In fact, you don't think you *deserve* love.'

'Shut up now, Pippa!' said Gunther, but his lower lip was starting to tremble. He didn't even bother to mime inverted commas.

'You zee, zat is an example. I zee it now in your brain, *ja*? Parts of it, they are for sure lighting up red. Because you are frightened to face the truth about yourself, zo you have lashed out at me!'

'I'M NOT FRIGHTENED!' shouted Gunther, sounding very frightened.

'Well, your brain is showing much activity in the fear regions. And also in the regions that show . . .' She peered more closely at him. '*Ach ja*. Loneliness. Sadness. And no-one-likes-me . . . ness.'

'LEAVE ME ALONE! STOP LOOKING INTO MY BRAIN! YOU . . . YOU . . . MARTIAN!'

He shouted this as he shot up from the table and

hurried out of the dining hall.

Pippa watched him go. Then she handed his plate, with his mash on it, back to Rahul.

'Hope you don't mind,' she said. 'One of the scoops might have some of Gunther's tears in it.'

CHAPTER 28

VERY DEADPAN

'Were you actually looking into Gunther's brain?' said Rahul on the way back to his flat after school.

'Yes. Once I stopped looking *for* Gunther's brain,' said Pip. 'It took a while to find . . .'

'Wow,' said Rahul, taking out his notebook. 'So the G-Glasses can give you like . . . X-ray vision?'

'Kind of. It's more like . . . once I've done the scan, I can see a simulated model of his brain, with all the areas of activity lit up.'

Rahul started scribbling this down furiously. Then he stopped and said: 'Pip. It was great what you did. Thank you. But – like with the hovering in the playground – I worry you might be drawing attention to yourself. And what you can do.'

Pip nodded. 'I know. But I can't stand bullying. I like the fact that here you get to meet people face to face. But I didn't realise it meant that some people would actually be horrible to others. Like beat them up and steal their food.'

'Yes, I'm afraid so,' said Rahul. 'Although people can also be horrible to other people *not* face to face. Online, I mean. Don't you have that?'

Pip thought about this. 'Yes. We do. But, because I don't know where they are, and never meet them, I'm not able to go and scan their brains to make them stop!'

Rahul laughed. Pip laughed too, but then her

face fell. 'Ow!' she said, clutching her tummy.

Rahul frowned. 'Maybe you should see a doctor . . .'

Pip shook her head. 'I don't see how we can do that without telling the doctor where I'm really from.'

'Hmm. You're right. Maybe we can find you some food that will be okay . . .'

By now they were standing outside the warehouse at Agarwal Supplies.

'Yes,' said Pip. 'Or maybe we really need to get that portal open.'

Rahul nodded and they went inside.

'Actually, I started to have an idea about that,' he said, flicking through his notebook. But he didn't get any further before his mum appeared from behind a shelf stacked with empty plant pots.

Holding Squeezy-Paws out in front of her. As far in front of her as she could.

'RAHUL! WHAT IS THIS CAT DOING HERE NOW?'

she said, thrusting the big ball of fur at her son.

'Meow,' said Squeezy-Paws, in a very, very dead-pan way.

CHAPTER 29

I'm calling a meeting

'A weird cat,' said Sanjay, appearing behind her. 'It says meow.'

'All cats say meow,' said Rahul.

'They don't. All cats *meow*. This one actually *says* meow. Like a human. Like you and I just said it.'

'Meow.'

'There! You see!'

'I don't care what comes out of the stupid-looking thing's mouth . . .' said Prisha.

'ME . . . OW!' said Squeezy-Paws.

'Hmm. You see, *there* it sounded genuinely offended,' said Sanjay.

'Just –' Prisha pushed the cat into Rahul's arms – 'get it back to whoever owns it.'

'It's . . . a . . . stray, I think,' said Rahul.

Sanjay laughed. 'It's the most well-fed stray I've ever seen.'

'Yes,' said Prisha, laughing. 'It's a chonk. An absolute unit.'

'ME-ME-ME-OWWWWWW!'

Rahul tried to stroke Squeezy-Paws's head to make her feel better. It didn't seem to work.

'Hello?' said Prisha, suddenly turning to Pip.

'Hello!' said Pip brightly.

'Do I know you?'

'This is Pip, Mum. A friend of mine from school . . .'

'Oh,' said Prisha. 'Do I know your parents?'

'Um. I don't think so . . .'

'Hmm. What's your surname?'

'@256X#YY.3_7.'

Prisha and Sanjay looked at her.

'Pardon?'

'@256X#YY.3_7.'

'She's . . . German!' said Rahul.

Pip blinked. *'Ja. Ich bin Deutsch.'*

Prisha frowned. 'That surname doesn't sound German. It sounds like . . . a password.'

'Quite a strong one,' said Sanjay. 'I might try and remember it for my online banking.'

'No, no, it's German,' said Rahul, pushing Pip further into the warehouse and away from his parents. 'She's related to the . . . Munich @256X#YY.3_7s! Lovely family. See you later!'

He went into the warehouse. Prisha looked at Sanjay. 'You need to speak to him. He's getting very weird.' Then she shouted, 'AND STOP MAKING SUCH A MESS IN THERE! DON'T LEAVE

TOILET SEATS ON THE FLOOR!'

'And definitely don't wee in them!' added Sanjay.

Prisha looked at him sternly.

'It was a joke,' said Sanjay sheepishly.

Once they got to where the toilet seat was, Rahul called a meeting. He actually said: 'I'm calling a meeting,' which was a bit unnecessary as the only people/animals who needed to be present were already there – Pip, him, Squeezy-Paws and Dag – but it made him feel more focused on the problem in hand: opening the portal.

But Rahul was interrupted by two things.

The first was Dag saying: 'Pip? Are you okay? You look a bit peaky.'

Pip grimaced. 'Yes . . . I think the food here doesn't agree with me. I like the taste, but I'm not sure I should be eating it.'

'Would you like some of my seeds?'

'No thank you . . .'

And the *second* thing that interrupted Rahul was a weird slapping noise coming from behind a shelf stacked with mismatched children's sandals.

He turned. 'What was that?'

'What?' asked Dag.

'Some kind of slapping noise,' said Rahul.

'I can't hear anything,' said Squeezy-Paws. Pip shook her head too.

Rahul listened more closely. 'Huh,' he said. 'Maybe it was just the wind.'

It wasn't, though.

CHAPTER 30

A weird thing to make up!

SLAP! SLAP!

'Will you be *quiet*, Gunther!' hissed Frank. 'Your breathing is so *loud*!' And he slapped him on the head again.

'Dad!' whispered Gunther. 'I think you're making more noise slapping me than I am breathing!'

'I am not. Your breathing sounds like we're in a wind tunnel. Like a *tornado*. Or a storm. Storm Gunther.' Frank narrowed his eyes. 'Although obviously we know the weather is secretly controlled by THEM.'

Gunther, not really understanding, but realising that the mention of THEM meant his dad was deadly serious, nodded.

'Sorry, Dad. I'll try to breathe more quietly.'

'Good.' Frank peered through a little gap in the shelves, which allowed him to see in between the mismatched children's sandals. 'Because I think Roool may have noticed something.'

'Raaoool.'

'Rah . . . ool?'

'I think it's –' Gunther screwed up his face – 'Raayol.'

Frank shook his head, as if it didn't matter. He put one eye up close to the little gap.

'I don't get it.'

'What?'

'We've come here, Gunther, because I started

to think you might be right . . . that that girl is an alien.'

Gunther looked very pleased. 'Yes?' he said.

'So. We've climbed in through the window and we've hidden here for three hours, waiting . . .'

'Well,' said Gunther, 'it took at least an hour of that for you to get through the window.'

Frank slapped Gunther on the forehead. 'Don't be rude!'

'I wasn't.'

'*Anyway* . . .' said Frank. 'We've been waiting for ages for her and –' he shook his head again – '*Royale* to appear.'

'Yes?'

'And now all they're doing is sitting round a toilet seat with a cat and a parrot.'

'Really?' said Gunther.

'Yes,' said Frank, moving away from the gap to stare crossly at Gunther. 'Why would I say that if it wasn't true? That would be a weird thing to make up!'

Gunther shuffled forward and put his eye to the gap in the shelves. He watched for a few seconds.

'Dad!' he whispered madly.

'What?'

'Get your phone out. Film this!'

'Why?'

'Because the parrot is talking!'

'Er . . . I don't reckon that's worth recording, Gunther. Even I don't think that means anything.'

Gunther looked round.

'Yeah. But so's the cat!'

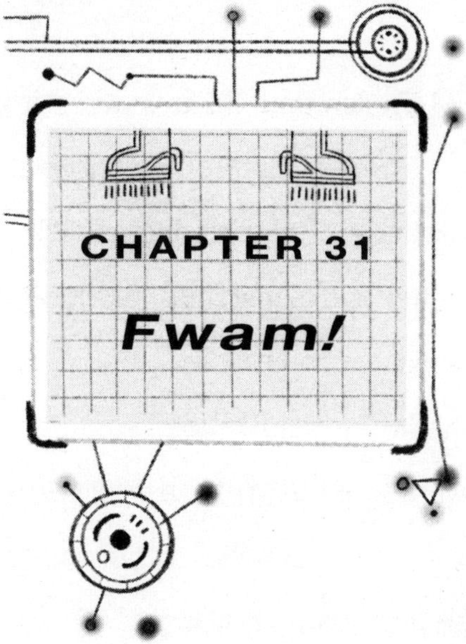

CHAPTER 31

Fwam!

'I hate that RoboClone!' Squeezy-Paws was saying. 'I always knew it was a bad lot.'

'You didn't,' said Pip. 'You loved it as long as it was feeding you. I even heard you purr once.'

'And cats don't even *do* that any more,' said Dag. 'In 3020, I mean.'

'Yes, well, we don't have to. We can just say, "Ooh, I like that, thank you."'

'So why were you purring then?' asked Pip.

Squeezy-Paws sniffed. 'I like to keep my paw in.'

'*Anyway* . . .' said Rahul. 'Tell me more about Pip 2. What, for example, is she made out of?'

'You call her she?' said Pip. 'Normally only I do that!'

'Well. She looks just like *you*,' said Rahul.

Rahul wanted to add: 'And you've become my friend. So when I saw that other version of you through the portal, I just thought, *Oh look, there's my friend*.'

But he felt a bit embarrassed at the idea of saying that. So he just said: 'Anyway. What is she . . . it . . . made of?'

'Not sure. Hold on.' Pip put on her G-Glasses. She blinked and the sides lit up. 'Okay, the model that Pip 2 is . . . it's mainly a skin-replicant polymer implanted with growth cells . . .'

'Yeah,' said Rahul. 'That doesn't mean very much to me. Does Pip 2 have any metal bits?'

The lights on the sides of the glasses flashed again. 'Yes. Her insides are a titanium-steel alloy,' said Pip. She took the glasses off. 'Why?'

'Well,' said Rahul, getting up and walking over to one of the warehouse shelves. He grabbed a box with a picture of a large magnet on it.

'If steel's involved, I just wonder if there's an invention I can make . . . using a whole load of these magnets to generate a very strong magnetic field. Maybe there's a way of getting our metal friend to open her end of the portal, then . . .'

He took the magnet out and held it in front of him in one hand. He lifted up his other hand and then slapped it sharply back on to the teeth of the magnet.

'. . . *Fwam!*' he said.

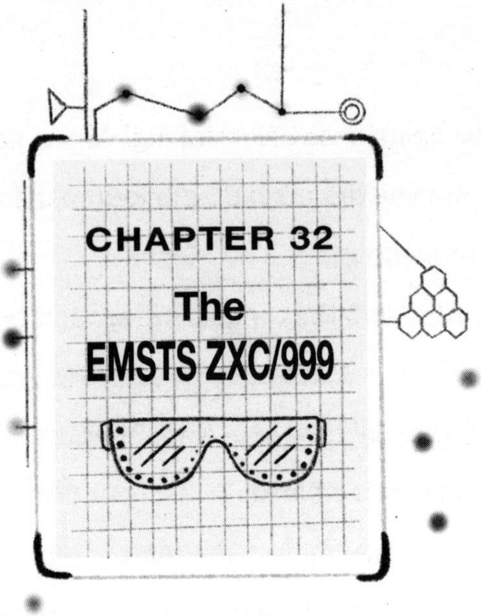

CHAPTER 32

The EMSTS ZXC/999

Rahul immediately started working on his invention. He drew up loads of plans in his notebook. He gave the invention a name: the Electro-Magnetic Space-Time Shuffler ZXC/999. This meant that Rahul *definitely* had his inventing mojo back now. Because he always used to give all his inventions long names, with random letters and numbers attached, to make them seem more like proper inventions.

He drew and drew. In its first draft, the drawings

of the EMSTS ZXC/999 looked like a sort of robot caterpillar, a long, bendy cylinder made up of about twenty magnets.

'Um . . . how are those sticking together?' said Pip when she saw the plans. She and Squeezy-Paws and Rahul were all bent over Rahul's notebook, with Dag hovering above them.

'They're magnets,' said Rahul.

'Yes. But you know that magnets *repel* each other.'

Rahul was silent for a moment. 'Yes,' he said.

'You didn't,' said Squeezy-Paws.

'Okay. Now I know less about science than a cat.'

'I know. Get used to it.'

'No, actually, I did know. But that's why it's called the *Electro*-Magnetic Space-Time Shuffler because –' and here he drew a circle round a wire coming out of the end magnet – 'I'm going to use *electricity* to reverse the polarity of the magnets.'

'Oh. Polarity is it now?' sniffed Squeezy-Paws.

'That's why magnets repel each other, Einstein. They have positive and negative polarities at each end. The positive end repels another positive end and negative, negative. So you need to change that to get them to stick together.'

'Yeah,' said Squeezy-Paws doubtfully. 'I knew that.' Then she looked at Pip and whispered (it's quite a thing to hear a cat whisper): 'Who's *Einstein*?'

'What are you going to use to change the polarity?' said Pip, ignoring Squeezy-Paws, but tickling her ear.

'These . . .' said Rahul, holding up what looked like two big pliers, a red one and a black one. They had wires attached.

'What are those?'

'They're called jump leads. You use them to restart car batteries.'

'Car whateries?' said Dag.

'Batteries. They're sort of boxes where electricity is stored.'

Squeezy-Paws sniffed. 'We have much more advanced ways of storing power in 3020.'

'Yeah, well, what you *don't* have is any ideas except this one about how to get back to 3020,' said Rahul.

Squeezy-Paws opened her mouth to say something clever, realised she couldn't think of anything, and shut it again.

'All we have to do –' he began drawing again – 'is attach one end to the battery in my dad's car. Then attach the other end to the EMSTS ZXC/999 and start the car. That should reverse the polarity throughout the system, making the magnets stick together!'

'It's a long shot, but it just might work!' squawked Dag.

'Where have you heard that phrase?' said Rahul.

'On an old film that was showing on one of the cracked TVs over there . . .'

'Right. Well, yes, Dag. It *is* a long shot, but it just might work.'

Pip looked up from the drawing. 'How long do you think it will take you to make?'

'A couple of days. Luckily, it's half term!'

'Okay,' she said, rubbing her stomach. 'As quick as you can, Rahul. Because I'm starting to feel hungry . . .'

'What's that?' said a voice. 'Hungry?'

'Uh-oh . . .' said Rahul.

It was Prisha. 'Why didn't you say! Come upstairs! Get out of this stupid warehouse! I've made loads of food!'

CHAPTER 33

Lederwhatty?

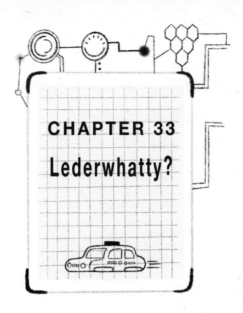

It was Friday night and Prisha always made a big meal. Tonight it was lamb Madras: spicy lamb curry.

She brought it out in an enormous pot, and heaved it on to the dining table where Pip and Rahul and Sanjay were seated.

'Oh no,' whispered Pip to Rahul. 'I'm so hungry. And this smells so delicious . . .'

'Hand me your plate, Pip!' said Prisha, plunging a spoon into the enormous pot.

'Um . . . sorry, Mrs Agarwal, but I don't normally eat this kind of thing . . .'

Prisha frowned. 'Curry?'

'Oh,' said Sanjay. 'Do we have any bratwurst, Prish?'

'What?' said Prisha.

'It's German for sausage.'

'Oh right. Perhaps you'd also like to offer her some beer and lederhosen?'

'Lederwhatty?'

Pip blinked. Her glasses flashed. 'Trousers. Short or knee-length leather breeches worn in German-speaking countries.' She blinked again. 'Goodness, they do look weird. Do all Germans – I mean do all *us* Germans – wear them?'

'Mum,' said Rahul, thinking it was best to cut in at this point. 'Pip's a vegetarian.'

'What's that?' asked Pip.

'Someone who only eats vegetables.'

'Oh. We don't have that where I'm from . . .'

'Germany,' said Sanjay, nodding. 'I believe not.'

'That's okay!' said Prisha, getting up. 'I've made tarka dhal as well!' She went into the kitchen.

'What's that?'

'Lentil curry,' said Rahul.

'Oh! I really love lentils. Well, I've never had real ones. I mean, the fake ones that our scientists create in laboratories—'

'In *Germany*,' said Rahul desperately.

'Yes! The German ones!'

'Sounds amazing,' said Sanjay, although he wasn't really listening. In fact, it was quite hard to hear what he was saying because his mouth was full of lamb Madras. Which was why he wasn't really listening. He wouldn't take any notice of anything anyone said now until he'd finished every mouthful.

'Here you go!' said Prisha, putting a slightly less large – but still pretty massive – pot on the table. Pip peered into it. The dhal was golden and simmering and smelled of spices and warmth and yumminess. Prisha doled out a large blob on to her plate.

Rahul shook his head. He took a deep breath and said: 'Listen, Mum . . . Dad . . . I don't think Pip can eat this either. Because . . . because . . .'

He paused. His parents looked at him.

Should I tell them the truth? he thought. *Will they just think I'm mad*? *Will they call the authorities*? *Will my dad just say 'that's nice' because he hasn't finished his Madras*? *What will happen to Pip*? *Will we both get into trouble*?

No, he thought, *the time has come. It's the best thing to do.*

'. . . because she's from the . . .'

'YUM!' said a voice next to him. 'That was SO delicious. Thank you!'

He looked round. Pip was sitting back in her chair, holding her stomach. Her plate was empty. Prisha smiled and took the plate away.

'Are you okay?' whispered Rahul. 'Are you going to . . . die?'

'I don't know,' said Pip. 'But it was worth it.'

CHAPTER 34
Oops

Pip didn't die, but when she woke up the next morning her stomach did really hurt. When the pain started to subside a little, Rahul suggested an experiment, to discover if there was ANY food from the present that wouldn't make her feel sick.

Well, not *any* food: any food he could find in the warehouse. Which meant Pip tried sweets, cheese sticks, tins of mushy peas and a type of Pot Noodle that was called Noodle Pot (admittedly, the food in the warehouse was a bit dodgy). He only gave her tiny amounts and wrote everything down in his notepad: he tried to make it as scientific a test as possible. And the results were clear: all the food from 2019 they could find made Pip feel sick.

'Do you know, I've really rather grown to like these,' said Squeezy-Paws, halfway through a bowl of cat biscuits. 'Obviously, I thought a cat of my evolved – and I do mean evolved – palate would not, but it turns out . . .'

'Yes, thanks, Squeezy-Paws,' said Rahul, looking worried.

'I'm certainly not eating those,' said Pip, halfway through trying a tiny bit of some biscuits that looked like – but weren't quite – Oreos. 'And neither should you. They're made of real cow.'

Squeezy-Paws looked up for a moment, concerned. Then she made an *ah well* face – which is quite similar to what a cat's face is like all the time

– and carried on eating.

Pip shook her head and spat out the bit of not-quite-Oreo. 'No. I can feel that's going to make my stomach hurt too.'

'Hmm,' said Rahul. 'I'm really worried about this. You haven't by any chance brought some food from your time with you?'

Pip thought for a second and then said, 'Oh! I forgot!'

She blinked. The ImageSuit shimmered back into its usual silver form. She put her hand into the central pocket and took out a tiny egg-shaped pill.

'What is that?' said Rahul.

'It's a boiled-egg-and-soldiers pill,' said Pip.

'Really? So everything in the future IS like it is in films! You eat pills that taste like whole meals!'

'Well, not normally. I normally have proper boiled egg and soldiers for breakfast. It's my favourite. Although the egg doesn't come from real chickens, of course.'

'Of course.'

'But when I was in my mum and dad's lab before I jumped into the portal I found these. They must have been developing them for taking with you on journeys through the transporter.'

She put her hand in her pocket again and took out another four pills. She held them out on her palm. Rahul couldn't resist. He popped one in his mouth.

'Oh my days!' he said. 'The egg's just how I like it. Half hard, half soft.' He rolled the pill round his mouth. 'And the toast . . . it's got butter on it!'

He swallowed and licked his lips. 'Amazing!'

Pip stared at him. 'Glad you liked it. Unfortunately, I was just holding them out to show you, not to give you one. As this may be the only food I can eat and now I've only got four left . . .'

Rahul stopped licking his lips. 'Oops.'

'Oops indeed,' said Squeezy-Paws.

CHAPTER 35

One-star rating

To be fair to Rahul, to make up for guzzling one of them, he did his best to help Pip stretch her egg-and-soldiers pills out over the new few days. Using a pair of nail scissors they found in something called *A Grooming Kit For Men*, he carefully cut the pills into a series of smaller meal-shaped pieces. Pip did complain on eating the first one that the way he'd cut them meant that she was getting only the egg half of the meal (and the soldiers later), but she accepted that this was an emergency.

At least it meant that they could spend a bit of time not worrying about food. Rahul was thinking hard about the Electro-Magnetic Space-Time Shuffler – he'd actually got all the magnets out of their boxes and lined up – but then, just before he actually started putting it together, Pip said: 'I want to see more of this time.'

'Sorry?'

'Well, if your plan and your invention work to get me back to 3020, that's great, but I think maybe this was quite a long way to come just to see –' she looked around – 'the Agarwal Supplies warehouse. And Bracket Wood School.'

'And Rahul's bedroom!' said Dag.

'And his dining room!' added Squeezy-Paws.

'Yes, okay. It's still a bit . . . limited.'

Rahul nodded. 'Yes. I think if TimeTripadvisor

exists in your time, it would only give this journey a one-star rating.'

'No!' said Pip, laughing. 'I've really enjoyed it. But maybe we could go on a few trips . . . ?' She looked at him. 'After all, I may not be going out of my house again for a very long time . . .'

Rahul put the magnet he was holding down. 'Good idea. I'll ask Mum and Dad.'

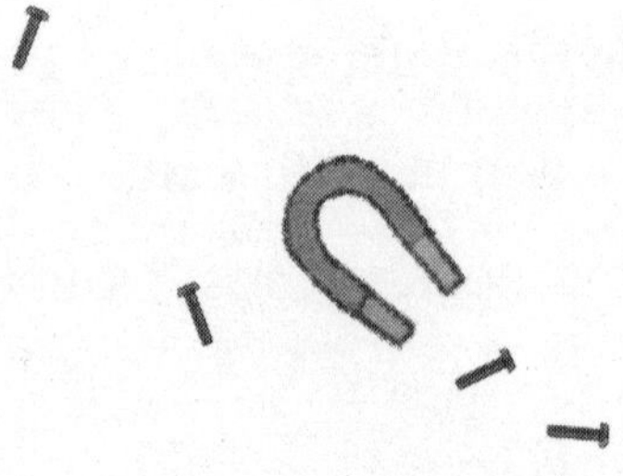

MONTAGE: LIKE IN FILMS

CHAPTER 36

Last one

Prisha and Sanjay, who were lovely parents really (Rahul had told them that Pip wanted to see some more sights before she went back to Germany . . .), said that they'd be glad to help plan some trips.

Luckily it was half term so, while Rahul continued to work in the evenings and in any spare time on the Electro-Magnetic Space-Time Shuffler ZXC/999, he and Pip went on some trips.

They visited a big museum where Pip could learn

even more about history, and actually see all the things she was interested in up close . . .

. . . although now going back a bit further than just the twenty-first century!

They went bowling, and scaled a climbing wall,

and played Laser Hunt, a game where you got to pretend you were living in the future, which went a tiny bit wrong when Pip changed her ImageSuit to *Reflect* and killed everyone who was playing at the time (not *actually* killed – just in the game!).

They went clothes shopping, although they didn't actually buy anything because Pip could just make her suit look like whatever they saw on the shelves. But they had fun confusing the other shoppers.

They even made it as far as the seaside. Pip had heard of the sea, and Miss Lucy had shown her videos of it, but it wasn't like seeing it properly. Because, it turned out, being at the sea wasn't only about seeing it. It was also about hearing the roar of it, feeling the wind from it and, above all, smelling the scent of it, salt and sand and seaweed, all mixed up like a perfume called LIFE.

'Oh! It's amazing!' said Pip, and ran towards the waves.

'Pip!' said Rahul. 'You can't just dive in! It's really, really cold . . . Plus, you can't swim! Can you?!'

But she did. She dived straight into the water. Rahul ran after her, throwing off his clothes, and dived in as well in his pants (and, unfortunately, socks – there wasn't time to take them off).

He was under the water for a few seconds: it was freezing and crashing and he couldn't keep his eyes open. He stood up on the sand, shivering, the seawater up to his chest . . .

Pip was also standing on the sand. Her ImageSuit had become a wetsuit, complete with goggles and snorkel.

'This is brilliant!' she said, smiling.

And lastly they went . . . to a football match. It wasn't the Stadium Above the Clouds – it wasn't even a Premiership game, just Bracket Wood FC playing their last game of the season – but it was in *a* stadium, and the match turned out to be really exciting, with Bracket Wood's top scorer, Johnny 'Five Chins' Johns, scoring a hat-trick and saving them from relegation to the LosingBet.Com League Division Five.

Rahul didn't know much about football, but he could tell Pip was enjoying herself. She shouted and cheered all the way through and, when Bracket Wood did their lap of honour at the end, she insisted on staying and clapping the players. In fact, they were the last two people left in the ground.

Johnny 'Five Chins' Johns noticed them as he went into the tunnel and gave Pip a thumbs up!

'Wow,' she said on their way out, 'that was worth travelling a thousand years across space and time by itself!'

'I'm glad!' said Rahul. 'Shall we get a burger . . . oh no. Sorry. I forgot.'

'It's okay,' said Pip. 'I've got more egg-and-soldiers pills left.' She reached into the pocket of her ImageSuit, presently configured to look like an anorak with a Bracket Wood shirt underneath (this had confused a few fans as no one wore Bracket Wood shirts because there was no club shop).

'Uh-oh!' she said.

'What?'

'Last one!' And she popped it into her mouth.

PART THREE

CHAPTER 37
Don't be ridiculous

Next day, Rahul called one of his meetings in the warehouse with Pip, Squeezy-Paws and Dag, although Squeezy-Paws was once again mainly just eating cat biscuits.

'Okay,' he said. 'I thought it was time to update everyone on how I'm getting on with building the machine to catch Pip 2—'

'The Electro-Magnetic Space-Time Shuffler ZXC/999?' said Pip.

Rahul frowned. 'You remembered the whole name?'

Pip nodded. 'I recorded it.'

'Pardon?'

'If something important happens, I can record it with my eyes. Well, the bit of my eyes that is linked to my brain chip, on which it's recorded.' She blinked and her eyes went blank, like she was watching something on the inside of them. 'Yes, that's definitely what you called it.'

'Did you just watch me saying it in the past?'

'Yes.' She blinked again. 'Oh! Then you start calling it the EMSTS ZXC/999 for short.'

Rahul laughed. 'Wow. I'm going to miss you, Pip!'

She smiled. 'I'm going to miss you too, Rahul. But only if you actually get me back to my own time . . . so that I *can* miss you. After all, I've *really* run out of food now.'

'Right! Yes. Okay.' He got up and went round the

back of the shelves, re-emerging seconds later with a magnet and a large torch.

'Oh,' said Pip. 'It looked a bit different in the drawings.'

'No. This is only part of it. You'll see. So. We need one of us in here to open the portal . . . then we have to get Pip 2 to open the portal at the 3020 end . . . but it all has to be timed perfectly because I don't think it's going to be open very long. I need to stay in here to make sure it all works, and obviously, Pip, you have to stay in here to be first through the portal . . .'

'Right . . .' said Pip. 'That all sounds easy enough?'

'Well,' said Rahul, 'except maybe for one thing. You remember what I said earlier about reversing the magnetic polarity? About using the battery in my parents' car for that?'

She nodded.

Rahul held up the jump leads and attached them

to the magnet. 'Okay. So. Once these are connected to the battery, we're going to need someone to turn on the engine.'

Pip frowned. 'Turn on the what now?'

'The engi— Okay, you don't have engines in your time. Make the car start.'

Pip frowned more deeply. 'So who's going to do that?'

Rahul looked up and Pip followed his gaze.

Dag was fluttering above them, practising flying somersaults.

'A parrot is going to start a car?' said Pip.

'Don't be ridiculous!' said Rahul. He looked at where Squeezy-Paws was still munching through biscuits. 'A parrot *and* a cat.'

CHAPTER 38

An inventor, not a planner

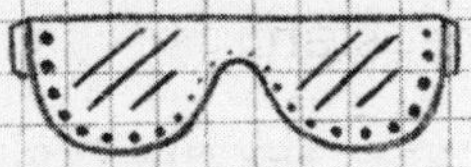

Sanjay and Prisha's car was an old one. It had been red once, but now it was mainly brown or, to be more exact, mud-coloured. Sanjay liked to say it was a 'people carrier', although it wasn't as big as cars like that. He called it that because it made it sound more impressive and also he thought it was fair enough, as a description, because the car did actually carry people.

Luckily, it was at least parked very close to the

door of the warehouse, which meant that attaching its battery to the Electro-Magnetic Space-Time Shuffler ZXC/999 via one set of jump leads was just about possible. Rahul had crept back into the flat where his parents had settled down in front of the TV, and borrowed – well, stolen – the car keys. He had used them to open the bonnet and then he'd attached the parts of the jump leads that looked like pliers to the positive and negative terminals of the car battery.

'Okay . . .' he said quietly and opened the door. 'In you get.'

Squeezy-Paws looked up at him. 'Are you *sure* about this?'

'No.'

Squeezy-Paws shrugged – as best she could, without really having shoulders – and jumped in. She sat on the driver's seat. Dag flew in and perched on the steering wheel.

'What's the plan, Stan?' he said.

'Rahul,' said Rahul.

'I know. It's just the sort of thing we parrots say.'

'Oh. Well. I'm going to go back up to the warehouse and – hopefully – me and Pip can get the other portal to open. Then I'll flash my torch at you – three times – to start the car.'

'Right,' said Squeezy-Paws. 'So basically you don't have a plan. I mean, how do *we* start the car? We don't have *hands*.'

Rahul shrugged. 'I'm an inventor, not a planner. You're a very sophisticated, very evolved cat. I'm sure you'll work something out.' He stuck the key in the ignition. 'You need to turn that, by the way. But NOT until you see my signal!'

With that, Rahul turned and shut the door.

CHAPTER 39

Pip vs Pip

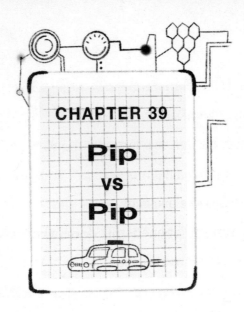

Pip and Rahul stood over the toilet seat. Rahul was holding the magnet and the torch.

'Okay,' he said. 'How are we going to get Pip 2 to open the portal in 3020?'

Pip stared at him. 'I thought you had a plan?'

Rahul looked exasperated. 'I just explained this to the cat. I invent stuff. I don't *plan* things.'

'Right,' said Pip. 'Wish you'd mentioned that before.'

'Well,' said Rahul, 'I'm also not from your time. I

don't know how to get a RoboClone that's become evil to do our bidding. I thought *you'd* know how to do that.'

Pip frowned. 'I don't know that Pip 2's become *evil*. I think maybe it's more to do with wanting to be treated more like a *human*.'

'Last time it opened the door when Dag sang down the portal,' said Rahul. 'But that won't work a second time, I don't think.'

Pip stared at him. 'What did you say?'

'That won't work a second time, I don't—'

'No. Before that. The first bit.'

Rahul thought. 'Er . . . last time it opened the door—'

'Yes! And what did I just say?!'

'Sorry, is this a short-term memory competition now?'

'I said that Pip 2 wants to be treated more like a human! More like a person! So, Rahul, are you ready? Is the EMSTS ZXC/999 all set up?'

'Um . . . well, it will be. Once I give the signal.'

'Okay!' said Pip. She bent over the toilet seat. 'PIP 2! PIP 2! ARE YOU THERE?' she shouted. Then, with a meaningful glance at Rahul, she added: 'Is *she* there? Does anyone know where *she* is? Has anyone seen *her*?'

Rahul and Pip stared into the blackness. Then, very slightly, there was a small crack in the dark: a tiny sliver of light appeared.

'Pip 2 . . . is that you? Is that *her*?' said Pip.

Rahul picked up his torch. Pip held up a hand. *Not yet.*

An echoey voice came through the darkness. 'This is not Pip 2!' it said.

'Oh,' said Pip.

'It is Pip. My name is Pip.' There was a pause. 'There is no Pip 2.'

Pip frowned. 'No!' she said towards the light. 'I'm Pip. You know I am.'

There was a pause. Then: 'I am Pip.'

'Oh, come on, Pip 2. Don't be like this. We've had lots of brilliant times together . . . Feeding Squeezy-Paws. Learning with Miss Lucy. Designing dreams for the DreamSet!'

There was another pause. 'That was all for *you*. Those were all things I helped you with! They weren't for *me*.'

'I'm not sure this is going that well,' whispered

Rahul. 'If what you're trying to do is win it – her – over . . .'

But Pip wasn't listening; she seemed to have got lost in the argument.

'I thought you were enjoying yourself!' she said.

'Well, maybe I did too!' came back the voice. 'But not any more!'

Despite the fact that Pip vs Pip – it was hard to say which one was 1 and which one was 2 now – seemed to be going quite badly, the crack, where the light showed through, *was* widening. Rahul decided that, even though he wasn't a planner, it was time to start the plan. He raised the torch and flashed it three times towards where his dad's car stood.

Nothing happened.

'I tried my best!' Pip was saying. 'I thought we were friends!'

'Not real friends!' the voice came back. And the crack widened again.

Frantically, Rahul flashed the torch again.

And again nothing happened.

CHAPTER 40

SUCK IT UP

'I mean, you have to agree, cat, that cats are clearly inferior. Now that we're here, it's obvious. In 2019, cats can only say meow. Whereas we parrots are speaking and—'

Knock! Knock! Knock!

Dag looked up. He was still perched on the steering wheel of Rahul's parents' car. The knocking was coming from the window. Behind the window was Rahul.

'*What on earth are you doing*?'

'Just having a chat . . .' said Dag.

Rahul shone his torch through the glass. 'Squeezy-Paws is asleep!' he said.

'Is she?' said Dag, looking down at the driver's seat. And there was Squeezy-Paws, curled up and snoring gently. 'Well, *that's* rude.'

'You were supposed to be looking out for the torch flashes!'

'No. *She* was supposed to be looking out for the torch flashes. But, as you can see, she's nodded off! Honestly! Cats!'

Rahul opened the car door. 'SQUEEZY-PAWS!' he shouted.

'Huh?'

'Oh, never mind!' He leaned over, shifted the gear stick to neutral – this is something you have to do to stop a manual car moving when it starts up – and turned the key. The car rumbled. He turned it again.

'AARGH! It won't start unless someone revs the accelerator pedal at the same time.'

'Well, can't you do it?' said Dag.

'No! I need to get back to the warehouse! As soon as the polarity switches!'

'Oh, for goodness' sake . . .' said Squeezy-Paws, now fully awake. She jumped down into the footwell and put both her front paws on the accelerator. 'Turn it on then!'

This time the engine started! Squeezy-Paws moved her paws backwards and forwards and the engine roared.

'Okay!' said Rahul. 'Keep doing that! Don't, whatever you do, touch the gear stick, though!'

He rushed back inside the warehouse to find Pip shouting down the toilet seat.

'LOOK! I GAVE YOU MY GRAVITYLESS BOOTS TO TRY OUT! YOU TOOK THEM OUTSIDE AND FLEW! WHICH I'M NOT EVEN ALLOWED TO DO!'

'YES!' the voice from the dark was shouting back. 'BECAUSE YOU'RE A HUMAN! RUB IT IN, WHY DON'T YOU?!'

At that point, the darkness widened enormously, as Pip 2 opened her end of the portal properly. The RoboClone appeared, staring triumphantly back at Pip.

'BUT IT DOESN'T MATTER ANY MORE. BECAUSE YOU'RE THERE AND I'M HERE! SUCK IT UP, PIP 2019! HA HA HA HA HA . . .'

Rahul knew it was now or never. He lifted up the other ends of the jump leads and attached them to the magnet. Immediately, he felt the pull of the magnet become more powerful. He held it tight as, from all over the warehouse, other magnets came flying.

They were coming from everywhere! Pip had to duck as three whizzed over her head! Rahul too had to bend down, but he held the magnet tightly as the others joined, flying in to stick to one another! In his hand, it grew, one magnet after another, to create a tunnel of magnets: the Electro-Magnetic Space-Time Shuffler ZXC/999!

He pointed it like an enormous magnet gun at the toilet seat.

'HA HA HA HA HA HA . . . Hey . . . what's happening . . . ?' said Pip 2. 'WHO – WHAT – IS PULLING ME INTO THE PORTA— AAAAAARRGGGHHH—'

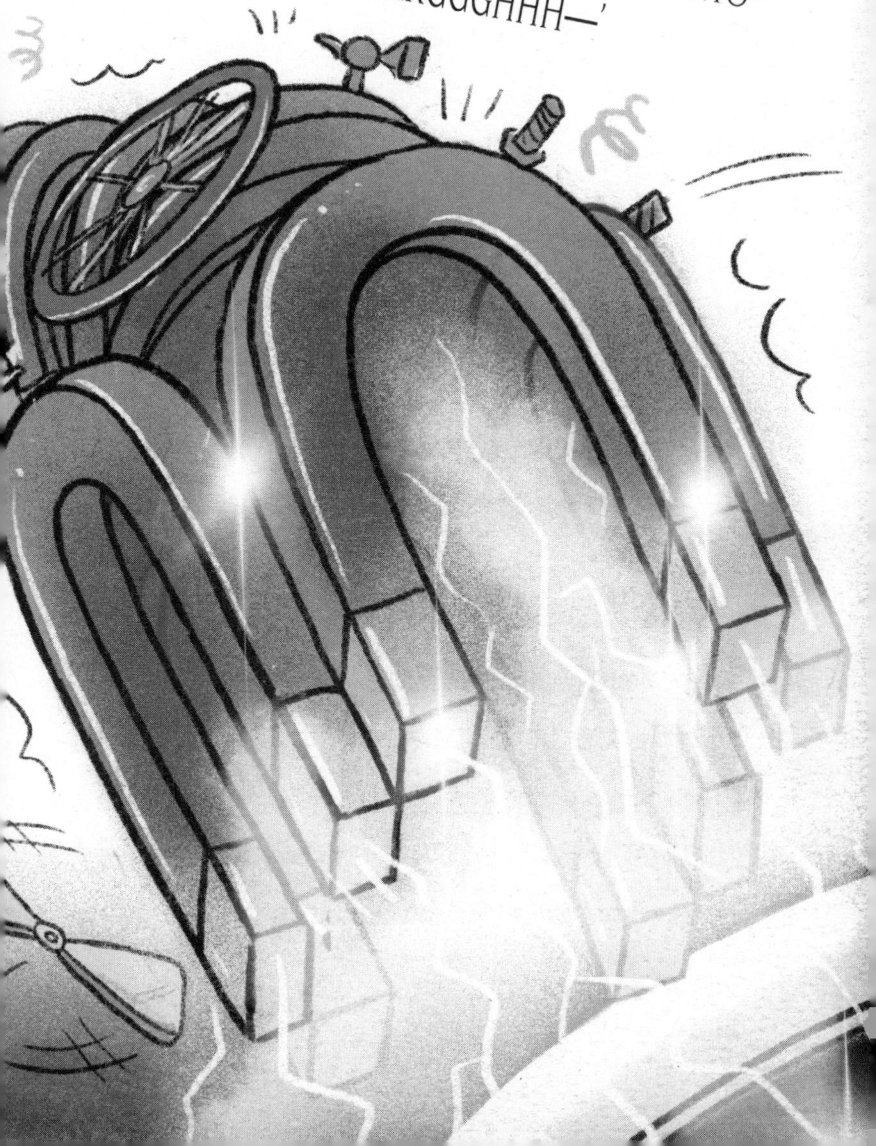

CHAPTER 41

Free

'—HHHHH!' screamed Pip 2, as she was sucked magnetically through to the other side of the portal. She emerged from the toilet seat and flew across the warehouse! She put her hands out as she went, and then *FWAM!* Both of them ended up stuck to the furthest magnet, the far end of the Electro-Magnetic Space-Time Shuffler ZXC/999!

'WHAT HAVE YOU DONE?' shouted the RoboClone.

'Welcome to 2019!' said Rahul. 'Blimey,' he added,

looking over at Pip. 'She really does look *exactly* like you.'

'I'm sorry, Pip 2—' said Pip.

'Pip!'

'Yes?'

'No, I AM PIP!'

'I AM!'

'Oh lordy,' said Rahul, looking between the two of them. 'Hey! Why don't we call Pip . . . BioPip, and you . . . RoboPip . . . ?'

Pip 2 looked unhappy. Not least because she was having to turn her body round awkwardly to face Pip and Rahul. It was a bit like she was handcuffed to the EMSTS ZXC/999.

'THAT, WHOEVER YOU ARE, IS WORSE!'

'Yes, but I think just for the sake of clarity . . .'

As he said this, BioPip began to move towards the toilet seat. She bent over it, preparing to dive in.

'I need to go, Rahul. Look . . .'

Rahul peered into the toilet seat. At the other

end of the tunnel, a small shadow of darkness was slowly moving across the oval of light. It was the door at the other end, the one left open when Pip 2 had been pulled through, starting to close.

She turned to Rahul to say goodbye. At which point, RoboPip looked at Rahul across the magnets and blinked twice.

'Oh no. Pip 2! Stop it!' said BioPip.

'What's happening?' said Rahul nervously. 'What's she doing?'

'Scanning you! Like I did to Gunther!'

RoboPip finished blinking and looked straight at him.

'So . . . Rahul Agarwal, I see you think of yourself as an inventor. And you have invented this . . . silly little magnetised caterpillar?'

'A silly little magnetised caterpillar that managed to drag you from a thousand and one years away, you mean?'

RoboPip sneered at this. But BioPip said: 'That's

good, Rahul! Keep going! Fight back! Resist what she says about you!'

RoboPip shook her head and smiled evilly.

'But you do know that whatever I say about you will be true, Rahul,' said RoboPip, leaning towards him. 'Because I am looking into *your brain*.'

'Right . . .' said Rahul, steeling himself, trying to meet her eye.

'And you do know that you are not *really* a great inventor, don't you? I can see in the sections of your brain where you keep your ego – the things about yourself you are proud of – that the last invention you were pleased with was that car, the one you built out of a wheelchair . . .'

'Yes.'

'But it has been a while since then, hasn't it? And your friend . . . Amy . . .' She peered, it seemed, deeper into his head. 'She looks nice, but she has gone and left you here.'

Rahul suddenly felt very sad. 'Yes . . .'

'Rahul!' said BioPip. 'Hold on! Don't let her get to you!'

'And now you are hoping that you have found a new friend here,' said RoboPip, gesturing towards BioPip. 'I can see how you desperately want that. But she is going to go, isn't she? Back to her own time. That is what your whole little

plan was meant to achieve after all.'

Rahul sniffed. 'Wasn't really a plan. I'm more of an inventor than a planner . . . Well, I thought I was . . .' He felt on the verge of tears.

'Do not cry, Rahul,' said RoboPip. She stared at

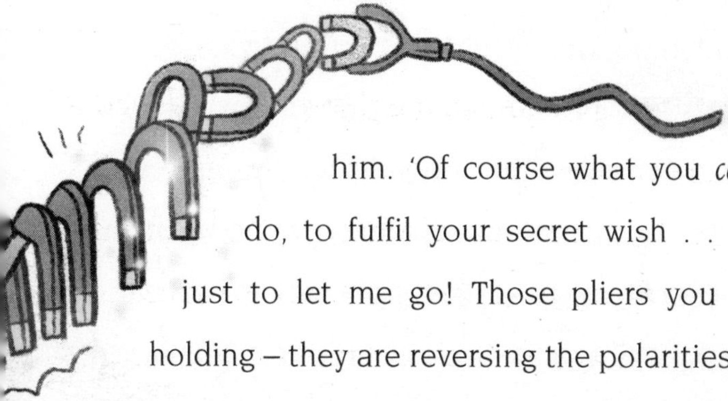

him. 'Of course what you *could* do, to fulfil your secret wish . . . is just to let me go! Those pliers you are holding – they are reversing the polarities on these magnets, aren't they? So, if you just take them off, your silly little magnetic caterpillar will fall apart, and I will go back into the portal and shut the door on the other side. And your new friend –' and here she turned, looking more evil than ever, to BioPip – 'well, she will be with you for ever!'

Rahul looked from RoboPip to BioPip. BioPip looked back at him. She wanted to say something – something that would make it all right, that, yes, she *was* going to dive into the portal and disappear forever, but that didn't mean . . . that didn't mean . . . No. She couldn't think of anything to make it better. She shut her eyes and shook her head.

Rahul looked down. He was still holding the jump lead that was attached to the first magnet of the EMSTS ZXC/999.

He knew everything RoboPip had said was true. He *did* want Pip – BioPip – to stay. He didn't want her to go. All he had to do was release the jump lead – as easy as releasing a pair of pliers – and RoboPip would be free: free to jump back and close the portal forever.

I don't know what to do, he thought. *I really don't know what to do.*

CHAPTER 42

Sill-ee

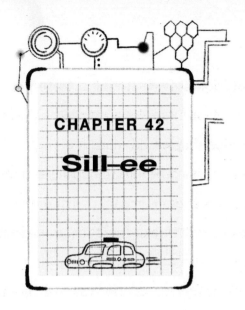

And then RoboPip was pulled sharply away from him. But not because he'd released the pliers from the magnet. In fact, Rahul didn't really understand what was happening. All he knew was that she was being pulled . . . and so was the EMSTS ZXC/999 . . . and so was he!

So that *we* can understand what was happening, let's go back in time. But not a thousand and one years.

About two minutes. To the car outside.

'How long am I meant to be revving this pedal?' asked Squeezy-Paws.

'I dunno,' said Dag. He was still perched on the steering wheel.

'I mean, I don't *mind* doing it. I used to do it as a kitten.'

'What?' said Dag. 'Rev pedals on old cars?'

'No, move my front paws backwards and forwards like this. I did it on my mum's tummy. For milk.'

'Urgh,' said Dag. 'Too much information.'

Suddenly there was a knock at the window.

'Ah, that'll be Rahul again,' said Squeezy-Paws.

'WHAT IS GOING ON?' shouted Prisha through the glass.

Now we have to go back another few minutes from there. To the flat above the warehouse.

'I don't know what's up with that boy at the

moment,' Prisha was saying, as she turned the TV off. 'Has he done his homework?'

'Oh, just don't worry about it, Prisha,' said Sanjay, getting up from the sofa.

'Hmm. The number of times you've said that. Like when he was making that wheelchair supercar . . .'

'Okay, okay. But he's a quieter boy now.'

'Yes. But is that good? Maybe he's depressed.'

'Of course he's not depressed!' Sanjay wandered over to the window to shut the curtains.

'And who *is* that German girl? She seems a little . . . strange. Since she's been around, in fact, *everything* seems a little strange.'

'Oh, don't be so sill—' said Sanjay.

Prisha looked up. He was staring out of the window. 'Ee?' she said.

'Pardon?' said Sanjay. His voice sounded strangled.

'Sill-*ee*. Don't be so sill-*ee*. About everything being

strange. I assume that's what you were going to say?' said Prisha, coming over to him.

'Yes,' said Sanjay, turning to her. He looked very worried. 'I *was* going to say that. Before I saw –' he looked out of the window again and pointed – 'our car being stolen by a parrot and a cat!'

CHAPTER 43
It's complicated

'WHAT IS GOING ON?' shouted Prisha (as I wrote earlier), knocking on the car window. 'WHY ARE THERE ANIMALS IN OUR CAR? WITH THE ENGINE RUNNING?!'

'Er . . .' said Dag.

'Oh dear,' said Squeezy-Paws.

'My goodness!' said Prisha, pulling at the handle on the driver's side. 'They've even locked the door!'

'Er . . . no, Prisha,' replied Sanjay. 'It's just a bit

sticky. I was going to fix it with some oil that we have in the warehouse, but, when I opened the canister, it turned out to be Ribena.'

She tutted and went round to open the passenger door. She got in and sat down in the back. Sanjay followed her. He looked at Dag, still perched on the steering wheel, and said: 'Are we there yet?'

'Sanjay! This is no time for jokes!'

'Sorry.'

She leaned over the front seats and looked down. 'This is incredible. Why is the cat revving the accelerator pedal?'

'It's complicated,' said Dag.

'AHA!' said Sanjay. 'I *knew* you could say more than Pretty Polly!'

Prisha stared at her husband. 'Okay,' she said. 'You just sit there and joke about this situation. *I'm* going to do something about it.'

She reached over and pulled the gear stick

towards her, putting the car into reverse.

At which point, it shot backwards.

Which led to . . .

CHAPTER 44
MUMMY AND DADDY

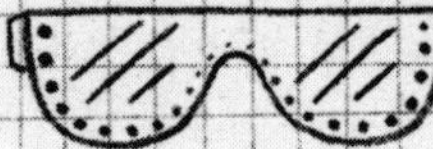

...RoboPip and the EMSTS ZXC/999 being pulled sharply away from Rahul!

And now we're back to where we were before.

The RoboClone's hands were still stuck to the magnets, and whatever was pulling it – well, *we* know what was pulling it, but Rahul didn't – was making her spin to one side of him!

'AAARRGGH!' shouted RoboPip.

Rahul wasn't strong enough to hold on to his

invention and had to let go. RoboPip, who *couldn't* let go, was being dragged along the floor of the warehouse!

'OW! OW! OW!'

'Is she actually in pain?' asked Rahul.

'Kind of,' said BioPip. 'She has sensors to simulate it anyway. But she may just be trying to make us feel bad!'

'I'M NOT! OW!' Then RoboPip blinked twice and rose into the air.

'What's happening now?' said Rahul.

'She's turned on her GravityLess Boots!'

'I thought they were *your* GravityLess Boots!'

'MUMMY AND DADDY BOUGHT ME MY OWN PAIR!' shouted RoboPip.

'THEY AREN'T YOUR MUM AND DAD! YOU'VE TRICKED THEM! PLUS, I NEVER CALL THEM MUMMY AND DADDY!'

'I DON'T CARE! THEY LOVE ME AS

MUCH AS THEY EVER LOVED Y— OW!' said RoboPip again, banging her head on the door of the warehouse, as she was pulled out of it.

Rahul and Pip looked at each other for a second and then followed her.

CHAPTER 45

The ‘Oh!’

Outside, they could finally see what was happening. Rahul’s parents’ car was being driven, backwards, apparently by Dag – well, not apparently, *actually* by Dag, whose claws were turning the wheel as he tried his best to steer – across the forecourt outside the warehouse.

The jump leads were coming out of the bonnet, and were attached to the EMSTS ZXC/999. Which was attached to RoboPip. Who was being pulled along while hovering a metre above the ground.

'That's something you don't see every day,' said Rahul (who, as I said earlier, had become a bit more joke-cracking than he used to be).

'Is that . . . your mum and dad in the back of the car?' said BioPip.

'Oh dear,' said Rahul. He could see them screaming and gesticulating from the back seats. He was glad he wasn't actually inside the car.

Then Sanjay wound down the window. 'RAHUL!' he shouted. 'IS THIS YOUR DOING?'

'It's complicated,' Rahul replied.

'THAT'S WHAT THE PARROT SAID!'

'Oh,' said Rahul. 'He's meant to just say *Pretty Polly*!'

'AAARGGH!' said Sanjay, as the same parrot swerved the wheel to the right.

'SORRY!' said Dag. 'BUT I DON'T KNOW HOW TO DRIVE! ESPECIALLY NOT BACKWARDS!'

'I think they might have worked out that Dag can speak,' whispered Rahul to BioPip. 'Anyway, Dad, what you need to do is . . .'

'HA!' shouted RoboPip. She had crossed her legs and was sitting grandly in the air. 'EVEN HERE, IN THIS PRIMITIVE PLACE, I AM ABOVE YOU, PIP! SEE HOW I FLOAT! I AM BETTER IN THE GRAVITYLESS BOOTS THAN YOU EVER WERE, EVEN DRAGGED ALONG BY THIS STUPID MACHINE ATTACHED TO THIS STUPID CAR AND— OH!'

The 'Oh!' was because, even though RoboPip had

been shouting and proclaiming from her high-flown position above them all, she hadn't quite managed to drown out what Rahul had been telling his dad, which was: *Just lean over and turn the engine off*.

Which Sanjay had done.

Which had meant that the polarity reversal on the EMSTS ZXC/999 had ended.

Which meant all the magnets had flown apart from one another and, although RoboPip might have been able to stay hovering in the air in her GravityLess Boots, two of them had banged into her face.

Which is why she said, 'Oh!'

And came crashing down.

CHAPTER 46

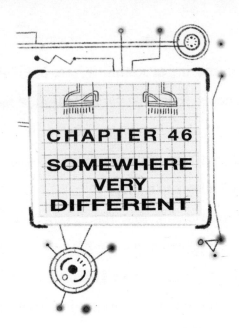

SOMEWHERE VERY DIFFERENT

A second later, RoboPip was sprawled on the ground. BioPip and Rahul rushed over to her.

'Is she okay?' asked Rahul.

'Well . . .' said BioPip, kneeling down. RoboPip was on her back. Her eyes were open, but there was nothing behind them. She looked for the first time like . . . well, like a robot. Like a robot that had been switched off. 'She might be broken. But I think maybe she was a bit before.'

She looked up at Rahul. 'In her head, I mean. RoboClones aren't meant to start thinking they're humans. She did need an upgrade . . .'

Rahul knelt down too. 'I know she's a machine, but I feel a bit sorry for her.'

He grabbed a piece of tarpaulin that was lying on the ground nearby and put it over RoboPip, covering her face.

'Yes,' said Pip (I think we can go back to just Pip now). She shook her head. 'Maybe if I hadn't just thought of her as a machine, back in 3020, none of this would've happened.'

They stood up. Dag flew on to Pip's shoulder. Squeezy-Paws padded up, settling by Rahul's feet. No one said anything. It felt like a little funeral for Pip 2. But Rahul suddenly remembered something.

'Um, Pip,' he whispered. 'This is all very respectful, but I don't think we've got time for a minute's silence.'

'Why not?'

'Because,' he said, looking over his shoulder at the warehouse, 'remember that the portal – back to your time – is closing! And, once it does, I don't know how – or if – we'll be able to get it open again!'

'How long have we got?'

Rahul shrugged. 'I don't know. It was closing slowly, but I don't know how portals work. Minutes, not hours, I think?'

'Okay, let's go,' said Pip. But then, as they turned to go back inside, Rahul's parents were there, waiting.

'Right,' said Sanjay. 'Enough already. It's time, Rahul, that you start telling us what exactly is going on.'

'Yes,' said Prisha. '*And* who exactly this Pip person is.'

Rahul looked at Pip. Pip shrugged. Rahul looked back at his parents.

'Okay. So, I know this is hard to believe, but Pip isn't from Germany.'

'Right,' said Sanjay. 'Given everything that's happened, that's not *that* hard to believe.'

Rahul took a deep breath. 'She's actually from—'

'SOMEWHERE VERY DIFFERENT!'

It wasn't Rahul who made this – VERY LOUD – statement.

They all turned. Standing behind them, between the car and the warehouse, was Frank Flackle. With him was Gunther, his arms crossed, smiling triumphantly. Behind them was a large group of people. There were some women and a few children, but it was mainly men, who all looked a bit like Frank Flackle. Actually, even the women and children looked a bit like Frank Flackle. They *all* had their arms crossed.

'I beg your pardon?' said Prisha.

Frank Flackle took out his phone, held it up

and clicked on it. There was a video on the screen, presently on pause. Prisha and Sanjay peered at it. Rahul, Pip, Dag and Squeezy-Paws didn't bother, as they could tell straight away that it was footage of them, round the toilet seat, talking.

Frank raised a finger. Then he realised he couldn't do the action he wanted to do while holding his phone.

'Hang on to this a second, Gunther,' he said, handing it to his son.

'Why?'

'Just hold it!'

'All right, *sorry*.'

Frank – free of phone – now put up both his hands, index fingers bent at the ready.

'"PIPPA",' he said, twitching those fingers triumphantly, 'IS FROM ANOTHER PLANET!'

CHAPTER 47
Flackle-alikes

A roar of approval went up from the large group of Frank Flackle lookalikes.

'What?' said Rahul.

'YES!' cried Gunther. 'MY DAD'S RIGHT!' Doing the inverted commas mime as well, although awkwardly, as he was now holding the phone, he said: '"PIPPA" . . . IS AN ALIEN!'

'Is she?' said Sanjay.

'Listen,' said Rahul, looking frantically at the

warehouse. 'We don't have time for all this!'

'We have to go!' said Pip.

'*Are* you?' said Prisha. 'An alien?'

'Oh my days . . .' said Rahul.

'No, I'm not!' said Pip.

'YOU ARE! WE ALL KNOW YOU ARE!' shouted Frank.

Another roar went up from the crowd behind him. Rahul noticed that it wasn't just a roar of approval. It was angry, aggressive. These people weren't just a crowd. They were a mob. They were after Pip. What they wanted to do with her, Rahul wasn't sure. Nor was he sure he wanted to find out.

'I saw you hovering in the air!' shouted Gunther. 'When you were playing football in the playground!'

'YES! YOU DID! AND SO DID I!' said Frank. Then he held up Gunther's hand with his phone in it. 'And we have *other* evidence as well . . .'

'Excuse me!' said Prisha, moving to stand in front

of the crowd of people. 'Who are *you*? And who are all these people who look a bit like you?'

'I . . . am Frank Flackle!'

'Well, that just sounds like stupid swearing.'

'I beg your pardon? It's my name!'

'It still sounds like stupid swearing.'

'Anyway!' said Frank, looking very cheesed off. 'Frank Flackle is who I am. And these –' he made a big sweeping gesture behind him – 'are all truth-seekers, like me. We all subscribe to SecretOPedia!'

'Secret-o-what now?' said Sanjay.

'It's a website. Where you can find out the truth. The real truth that THEY don't want you to know.'

'Who's they?' said Prisha.

'THEY!' yelled Gunther.

'Just shouting it isn't an explanation.'

'THEM!'

'Nope. Still doesn't help.'

'Anyway!' said Frank. 'I filmed your son, Mrs Agarwal, and "Pippa"—'

'Why do you keep doing that with your fingers?' asked Sanjay.

'And I saw those . . . animals there – that parrot and that cat – *talking*! Like humans! I then relayed that information to all my fellow truth-seekers! Who came in search of the truth! THAT is why we're all here. Because clearly they're all ALIENS!'

Another roar went up from the Flackle-alikes. Rahul noticed they'd all taken their phones out and were filming the scene. Prisha turned to Rahul.

'Can you explain, Rahul? I can't say I like this man's tone much, nor the fact that he's brought all his strange-looking friends on to our forecourt, but something very weird IS going on . . .'

Rahul nodded. 'Well, I'm not sure I can explain. I think there's only one person who can. And that's

Pip herself.' He turned round. 'Pip?'

Then he said it again: 'Pip?'

Then he – and Prisha and Sanjay, and even Gunther and Frank – said: 'Where's she gone?'

CHAPTER 48

Surely no one was going to believe this?

Pip was nowhere to be seen. Rahul spun in a circle, looking for her. Then he stopped three-quarters of the way round. He could see into the warehouse and, if he squinted, just about to where the toilet seat sat in the middle of the floor between two sets of shelves.

The portal was still open. *Oh*, he thought, *of course. While we were all talking out here, she must have snuck off and dived into it and gone . . . home. Back to 3020.*

Rahul was glad Pip was safe. He was glad she wasn't going to be set upon by Frank Flackle and his mob. But he was also sad that she'd just gone without even saying goodbye. And also – he looked up and realised that everyone was staring at him – Rahul was frightened. Because now she'd left him here on his own, having to explain it all by himself.

'Well, Rahul?' demanded Prisha.

'Um . . . Okay, well . . . Pip is . . . was . . . is—'

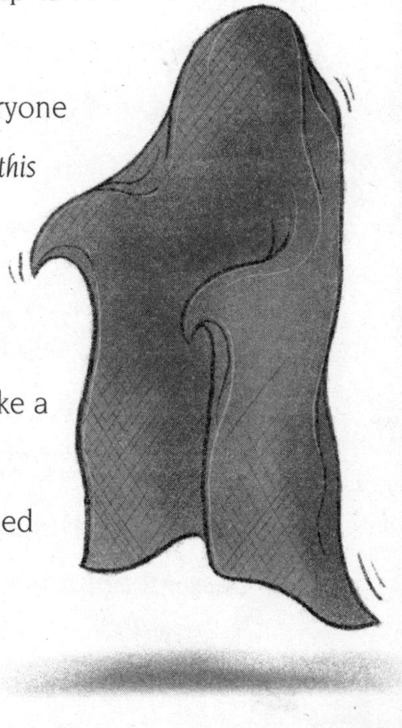

'Here!' said a voice. Everyone stared, confused as to where *this* voice had now come from.

The tarpaulin that had covered Pip 2 had got up and was standing by itself, like a black tarpaulin monster.

'AAAARGGGHH!' screamed everyone and backed away.

'Oh!' said the tarpaulin, and it fell off. Revealing . . . Pip 2. Not broken! Up and talking again!

'But it's true that I'm not a human being,' said Pip 2.

Rahul frowned. What was going on? Why was Pip 2 being nice and helping out?

'I KNEW IT!' said Frank Flackle.

'SO DID I!' said Gunther.

'I'm a robot,' said Pip 2. 'Look.' Her hand came up and touched her face. It seemed to tap her forehead in some complicated way, and then it revealed, inside, a host of wires and electric cells.

'AAAARGGGHH!' went everyone again.

'AAARGGH!' shrieked Gunther specifically. He was terrified.

'AAAARGGH!' said Frank, also terrified.

'Don't be frightened!' said Pip 2.

'I AM FRIGHTENED! DAD!' wailed Gunther.

'SO AM I, GUNTHER!'

'Okay, I'll put it back again. Hold on,' said Pip 2,

and smoothed her forehead back to normal. 'So. Yes. I'm a robot. And –' she came over to stand by Rahul – 'I was made by Rahul! He's a great inventor. Aren't you?'

'Er . . . I am?'

'Yes! Of course you are! And you *made* me. You designed me and then you built me! To a very high spec! I am one of the most advanced robots ever made in the twenty-first century. Which is why, Gunther, I have a built-in gravity-defying function in my boots, and it allowed me, when you threw yourself at me in the playground during football, to do this . . .'

And, with that, Pip 2 rose a metre into the air and hovered there.

'OOooooooOOOO!' went the crowd.

She floated back down to the ground.

'It's only momentary of course. I'm sure in time GravityLess Boots will be developed that allow you to do that for much longer.'

Sanjay walked over to Pip 2. He looked her up and down. He turned to Rahul. 'You built this, Rahul. Out of things you found in the warehouse?' he said.

'Yes!' said Pip 2.

Before Rahul could say, *No. I mean look at her – she's clearly made out of incredibly sophisticated parts. The warehouse mainly contains old cans of own-brand pet food, jump leads, five-litre Ribena bottles and plant pots,* Pip 2 continued, perhaps herself thinking this was a bit far-fetched, 'And a few other bits and pieces he found in other places.'

Rahul frowned. Surely no one was going to believe this?

'Wow,' said Sanjay, turning to the crowd and raising

his arms in the air. '*I knew* it! My son is a genius!'

Rahul looked at his mum. She was going to shoot it down, he knew.

'Well done, Rahul!' said Prisha, beaming. 'Wow! She looks so real!'

'HOLD ON!' said Frank Flackle. 'WAIT A MINUTE! ARE WE MEANT TO BELIEVE THIS?'

Rahul looked at him. This *wasn't* where he was expecting the disbelief to come from.

'Don't you sort of . . . believe anything?' he said. The crowd behind Gunther murmured.

'Well, yeah . . .' one of them said.

'That *is* true,' said another.

'I mean, I believe that most Premier League footballers are secretly made of carrots,' said someone else.

'I believe that snails have fourteen thousand teeth and some of them can kill you!' said a man at the back.

'No, that is actually true,' said Rahul.

'Oh no!' said the man. 'Now I'll have to hide from the killer snails!'

'SHUT UP!' shouted Frank. 'NEVER MIND WHAT WE NORMALLY BELIEVE! I STILL THINK SHE'S AN ALIEN! WHAT ABOUT –' he pointed to Dag, who had flown on to Pip 2's shoulder, and Squeezy-Paws, who had sat down at her feet – 'THE "CAT" AND THE "PARROT"?'

CHAPTER 49
Say something!

Just to be clear, Frank had mimed inverted commas round 'CAT' and 'PARROT'. Obviously.

'*What* about them?' asked Pip 2.

'Are they robots as well?' added Gunther.

'Yeah, did *Roool* make them too?' said Frank.

'Rahul,' said Rahul.

'Roo-hill?' said Frank.

'Or . . .' said Gunther, 'are they *aliens* in cat and parrot form?'

'Don't be ridiculous!' said Pip 2. 'They're a cat and a parrot!'

'They really are,' said Rahul.

'Well then, how do you explain *this*!' said Gunther, looking round at the crowd and holding up his dad's phone. He clicked on it and a video started to play. The video, to be exact, that Frank had filmed of Squeezy-Paws, Dag, Pip and Rahul in the warehouse.

'Now. Everybody watch! Let's hear what this parrot and this cat . . . SAY!'

The mob all crowded round Gunther to look up at the phone. Rahul and Pip 2 and Prisha and Sanjay – and even Dag and Squeezy-Paws – did so as well. Everyone was looking at Frank's phone. It showed a shaky sequence as he tried to focus on the two animals.

Pip could be heard to say: '*You didn't. You loved it as long as it was feeding you. I even heard you purr once.*'

And then Squeezy-Paws, on the film, looked up and said: '*Meow. Meow, meow, meow. Meoooowww!*'

She glanced at Dag who said: '*Pretty Polly! Pretty Polly! Pretty Polly!*'

It continued.

'*Meow!*'

'*Pretty Polly!*'

'*Meow!*'

'WHAT'S GOING ON?'

This wasn't either animal. Nor was it on the film. It was Frank Flackle, who was staring desperately at his phone.

'Well,' said Rahul, 'it looks like . . . a cat is saying *Meow*. And a parrot is saying *Pretty Polly*.'

'I know! But, when I recorded it, they were saying all sorts of other stuff! They were talking like . . . people! Weren't they, Gunther?'

'Yes, Dad!'

During this conversation, Rahul noticed that

Sanjay had put his hand up, as if desperately wanting to add something to this conversation. Rahul sauntered over to him and gently put his dad's hand down, shushing him as he did so.

'Really?' said Pip 2. 'Or were you just hearing me and Rahul speaking and *thought* it was the animals? I mean, it looks like you *were* filming from quite a long way away behind some shelves . . .'

There was a murmur behind Frank. A murmur saying, 'Actually that sounds about right . . .'

And, 'Yes, that probably is what happened . . .'

'NO! THEY'RE ALIENS!' shouted Frank. He bent down to the cat. 'Say something! Say something –' he looked up at Pip 2 – 'what's its name?'

'Squeezy-Paws.'

'SAY SOMETHING, SQUEEZY-PAWS! SAY SOMETHING!'

Squeezy-Paws looked up at Frank Flackle and said, in her most deadpan, ironic voice, 'Meow.'

And everyone – Prisha, Sanjay, Rahul, Pip 2, even the crowd behind Frank, although actually not Gunther – laughed.

CHAPTER 50
A tiny bit more time

A few moments later, once Frank Flackle and his gang had shuffled off, the sky burst and rain came down in buckets. Everyone who was left ran for cover.

Sanjay and Prisha got in the car.

Rahul and Pip 2 ran to the warehouse.

For now, they were alone.

'Oh!' said Rahul. 'That was so funny. The way Gunther's dad straightened after speaking to the cat and walked away, trying to look dignified.'

'Yes!' said Pip 2. 'And then his son stood there for a bit and said, "Dad! Wait for me!"'

'And then nobody knew what to do for a bit and eventually just left . . .' said Rahul.

'Yes!'

Rahul stopped laughing. Then he looked at Pip 2, and said: 'So here's the thing, Pip . . . 2. You seem to have become much nicer. Since your bang on the head . . .'

Pip 2 smiled. 'Have I?'

'Yes. And here's another thing. Just now . . . when you hovered in the air for a bit and said to Gunther, *"I have a built-in gravity-defying function . . . and it allowed me, when you threw yourself at me in the playground during football, to do this . . ."*'

'Yes?'

'Well, Pip 2 wasn't *there* when that happened. Only Pip . . . 1.'

There was a short pause. Pip 2's face seemed to

go blank. Then, behind her, the light shimmered and, seconds later, another Pip appeared, holding the first Pip's arms from behind.

'Hello, Rahul . . .'

'Hello, Pip. It was *you* all the time, wasn't it?'

She nodded.

'Let me just work this through,' said Rahul. 'When everyone was on my case about what was going on, and I said, "Pip will explain," and I turned to you and you weren't there – I thought you'd jumped back into the portal. But you hadn't – you'd activated your ImageSuit to *Invisible* . . . ?'

Pip smiled. 'Yes. You were right. When you said we should save the power for a time it might really be needed.'

'I . . . was . . . ?'

'You're very clever, Rahul,' said Pip.

Rahul blushed. 'And then, after that, you were . . . *operating* Pip 2?'

'I was. I was holding her up and working her like a puppet basically. Because,' she said, holding the RoboClone up, 'she's broken.'

Rahul nodded. Pip put Pip 2 against the wall, where she stood motionless.

'What about Gunther's little film?' asked Rahul.

'Oh,' said Pip. 'That's easy. I just hacked into his phone through my MindLink. Then I overlaid what Dag and Squeezy-Paws had been talking about with some audio I'd recorded of them saying *Meow* and *Pretty Polly*. Which luckily they've both said quite a lot since I've been here.'

Rahul stared at her. 'And you could do all that from your . . . brain basically?'

'Well, using a chip inside my brain. I am from 3020, remember.'

'I do remember!'

Pip looked over at the toilet seat and her expression changed. She looked at him seriously. 'And, on that note, Rahul . . . it's been amazing . . . and I've survived longer than I might have here, thanks to the egg-and-soldiers pills . . . but I think I need to go home.'

Rahul felt a bit sad inside, but nodded.

'I understand,' he said. He peered into the toilet seat.

'The portal's still open. More shut than it was, but I don't think that will be a problem.'

Pip nodded. 'How much longer?'

Rahul looked inside. 'I dunno. It doesn't seem to be moving at all at the moment . . .'

'Hey!' A voice came through from the other end. 'Nina!'

'That's my dad!' said Pip.

'Nina, have you seen this? The portal's open.'

'What? The time-travel one?'

Rahul looked into the dark. He could see the shapes of two people moving at the other end.

'That's bad!' said Pip's mum's voice. 'Can you fix it?'

A hand appeared at the edge of the portal. 'It's stuck. I'll go and get a screwdriver . . .'

'Screwdriver?' said Rahul.

'*Sonic* screwdriver,' said Pip.

'Oh no. He's going to shut it!'

'Yes!' said Pip. 'No!'

'Hang on!' said Nina. 'I think we should go and find Pip first. Just to make sure she hasn't fallen into it, or anything.'

'Goodness,' said Ivan. 'That would be awful. Imagine our daughter finding herself who knows where in time or space!'

'Yes. I'm worried now. Let's go and check she's okay.'

The shapes moved away from the portal.

'Phew,' said Pip.

'Yes, phew,' said Rahul. 'They won't be able to find you. And Pip 2's here. So that means they'll be gone for a while . . .'

'Which . . .' said Pip, 'gives us a tiny bit more time.'

'I guess,' said Rahul.

Pip smiled at him. 'What's your shoe size?'

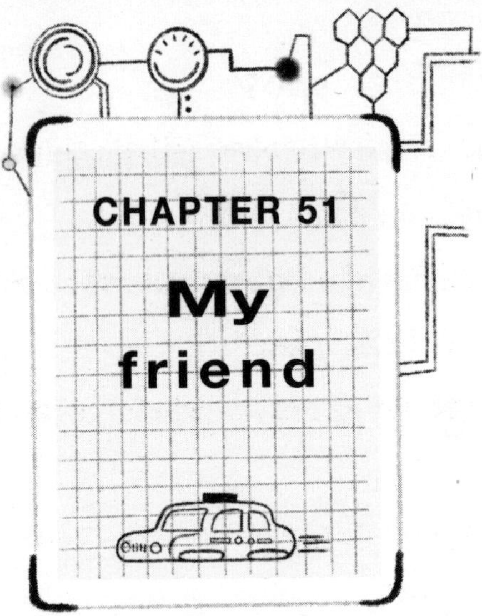

CHAPTER 51

My friend

Pip and Rahul stood on the forecourt, near the entrance to the warehouse. They both had GravityLess Boots on. Pip 2's fitted him remarkably well.

'Is this going to be okay?' said Rahul.

'I don't know,' said Pip. 'But in my own time, because I can't go outside, I've never been able to use my GravityLess Boots properly. And all I've done here with them is hover over a football match in a playground for a few seconds. That seems a bit of a waste to me.'

'Yes,' said Rahul. 'But you still *have* used them. I haven't. Will I be . . . okay?'

Pip was about to answer when Sanjay suddenly appeared.

'Hello, Rahul. Going in the warehouse for more amazing inventing, are we?'

'Er . . . yes, in a minute, Dad.'

'Hello . . . Rahul's amazing robot!'

'Hello, Mr Agarwal,' said Pip.

'Still *so* impressed, Rahul,' said Sanjay. 'She really seems almost human!'

'Yes,' said Rahul. 'It's amazing.'

He smiled and was about to go, but then turned back.

'Oh, by the way. Just one thing about recent . . . events . . .'

'Yes?'

'The cat. And the parrot.'

'Oh. Yes.'

'Um. Well. They did . . . kind of . . . *speak*. Like that rather unpleasant Flackle fellow was saying. I heard them when they were in the car.'

'Did they?'

'Yes. Your mother saw – and heard – it too. Not just the parrot, even the cat as well!' He looked at Rahul. 'Bit . . . weird?'

Rahul nodded. 'Dad. It's Saturday night.'

'Yes?'

'And you and Mum always have a glass of sherry on a Saturday night. Don't you?'

'Well . . .'

'Sometimes two glasses.'

Sanjay looked slightly embarrassed. He gestured towards Pip, as if to say, *Not in front of our guest, Rahul.*

'Dad. She's a robot,' said Rahul. Even though she wasn't.

'Oh. Yeah.'

'So. Did you have two glasses of sherry earlier tonight?'

Sanjay nodded. 'Three actually.'

'Okay. Maybe that had something to do with it?'

Sanjay carried on nodding. 'Maybe. Well, anyway . . .' He patted Pip on the head. 'Keep up the good work!'

'I will,' said Rahul.

'Really feels like actual hair!' Sanjay said over his shoulder as he made his way back to the flat. 'Incredible!'

'Yeah. Bye now!'

Pip was laughing. 'I'm going to miss your dad too,' she said. 'Now. What were you saying?'

'I was saying that I've

never used GravityLess Boots. Will I be okay?'

Pip smiled at him and held out her hand.

'Hold on to me, my friend.'

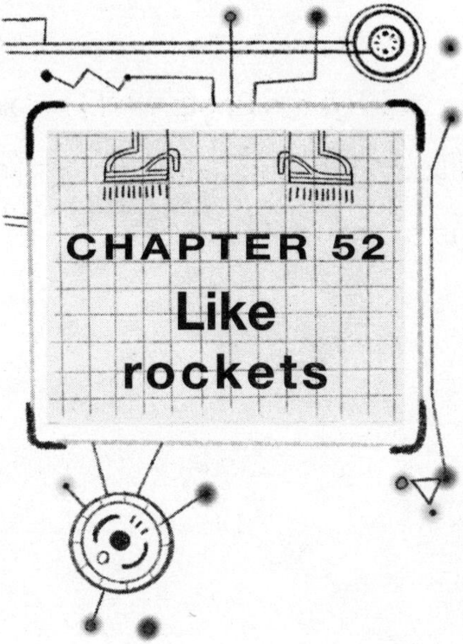

CHAPTER 52
Like rockets

When they first took off, Rahul was frightened. So, in truth, was Pip, who, as she said, had never used her boots outside before. At first, then, they hovered just a metre off the ground, holding hands like two paper cut-outs suspended in the wind. After a while, they grew bolder and, led by Pip, went upwards. They flew low over the roofs, past the lit windows, darting up or down at the last minute when the people inside peered outside.

Then they exchanged glances and soared. They flew high above the city. Looking down, everything was twinkling. *So* twinkling, in fact, it was sometimes hard to tell the difference between the city lights and the stars. Now she was confident, Pip insisted that they didn't just fly in a straight line: they rolled

with the wind; they swam through the clouds; they swooped and soared and turned somersaults in the night air. They even let go of each other's hands and free-styled across one another, like they were synchronised swimmers in the sky.

'This is the best fun I've ever had!' shouted Rahul,

as they hovered about thirty metres above Agarwal Supplies.

'Even more than when you rode in the Taylor TurboChaser?'

'Ha!' said Rahul, pleased that his new friend knew him so well. He thought about it. All he could tell was he hadn't been this happy since then. 'Well. It's certainly up there!' he shouted.

'*We're* up there!' said Pip. And twirled round with her arms out like a human rocket copter!

They were joined, eventually, by Dag.

'This is a bit high for me, to be honest, guys,' he said. 'I mean, the flying here's been very, very good, but I think I prefer to stay low. In the end, I may even prefer a good old perch.'

'So . . .' said Pip. 'Why have you come up here?

'Well,' he said, 'a little bird told me we were going home . . . like now.'

'A little bird?'

'Okay, a fat cat.'

Pip smiled. 'Yes, Dag, we are. We'll follow you down.'

Dag nodded and turned his outstretched wings towards the ground. Pip looked at Rahul and, through the rushing wind, shouted: 'Shall we go?'

Rahul smiled. He took his hand away from hers, adopted a diving pose and said: 'Let's go!'

And they both headed down, like rockets.

CHAPTER 53

A memento

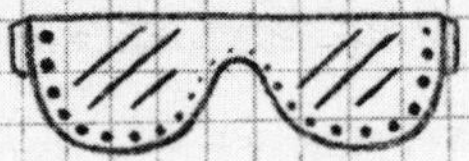

They stood, Rahul and Pip, on either side of the toilet seat. Rahul looked down. He could see, through the blackness, a ring of light: the portal was still open. He also, not for the first time since this had all started, wondered whether it felt quite right that this whole incredible adventure centred round an extra-large toilet seat.

'Okay . . .' said Pip. 'I guess this is it.'

'I guess,' said Rahul.

Pip blinked twice. Dag flew and Squeezy-Paws ran (as fast as she could) to join her.

'You ready to go back to 3020, guys?'

'I am!' said Dag. 'I'm an intelligent bird and I need to be able to express myself more than just . . .' He threw his beak back and screeched: 'Pretty Polly! Pretty Polly!'

'I thought you told Miss Lucy that that phrase had more meaning in it than humans thought.'

'Yeah. That was a lie.'

'And I,' said Squeezy-Paws, 'would just like to go home.'

'You haven't got a reason?' said Rahul.

Squeezy-Paws shook her head. 'Since I've been allowed to go outside, I've noticed something: sometimes I really, really want to go outside, but then as soon as I'm there I really, really want to come back in again. It's a bit like that.'

'Thank you for that, Squeezy,' said Pip. 'Tell you

what, animals. You two go first and I'll follow.'

'Okay!' said Dag. 'Bye, Rahul!'

'Bye, Dag!'

And the parrot flew into the toilet seat.

'Okay!' said Squeezy-Paws. 'Bye, Roool!'

'Rahul!'

'I know. It's a joke at the expense of those silly blokes who couldn't say your name. Bye, Rahul.'

'Bye, Squeezy-Paws!'

And the cat jumped into the toilet seat. Well, she couldn't quite get in there in one go, so she heaved herself on to the edge and then kind of furrily slid into it.

Pip and Rahul looked at each other again.

'It's been lovely to meet you, Rahul,' said Pip.

'You too, Pip. I hope you enjoyed your time in 2019!'

'It's been brilliant! Even though we're a thousand years ahead, there's loads of things about your time that are fantastic! The fact you can go outside! The air, the sky, the trees, the people . . . your family. You. I'm going to miss you very much.'

Rahul looked back into the portal. 'Maybe . . . when your mum and dad get the time machine right . . . without explosions . . . maybe you'll come back?'

Pip looked at him. A small tear appeared in her eye. 'I don't know. Perhaps. But we'll always be friends. Won't we?'

'I hope so,' said Rahul, his lower lip trembling. 'Oh!' he said, pleased to be able to focus on something that allowed him not to cry. 'I thought you could have this. As a memento.'

He handed her a scarf. It was a Bracket Wood FC one, from the game they'd watched together.

'I know they're not the City Cardinals. But if you ever do make it to the Stadium Above the Clouds . . .'

Pip smiled. 'I'll hold this up and cheer for Johnny Five Chins!'

Rahul laughed and Pip joined him. Then they stopped. It felt a bit awkward, like it does when two people have to say goodbye but can't quite get round to it.

'So. I'm going to take a little run-up and dive in,' Pip said eventually.

'Okay!' said Rahul.

She started to turn round, but he reached out and touched her on the shoulder.

'Just one thing. One thing I didn't say when we were going through about how you fooled Gunther and his dad and all those people . . .'

'Yes?' said Pip.

'Did you really think everyone would believe that I'd made . . . Pip 2? That I had made an amazing robot?' Rahul shook his head. 'You said it so confidently!'

Pip looked at him. She took his hand. 'Yes,' she said. 'Because you so obviously *are* an amazing inventor. You just *are* going to be one of the greatest inventors ever. I knew it then and I know it now . . .'

Now Rahul was crying. But he was smiling too.

'Thank you, Pip.'

She squeezed his hand. 'Goodbye, Rahul.'

'Goodbye, Pip.'

Then, without even taking her little run-up – perhaps because her eyes were too full of tears – she dived into the toilet seat and was gone.

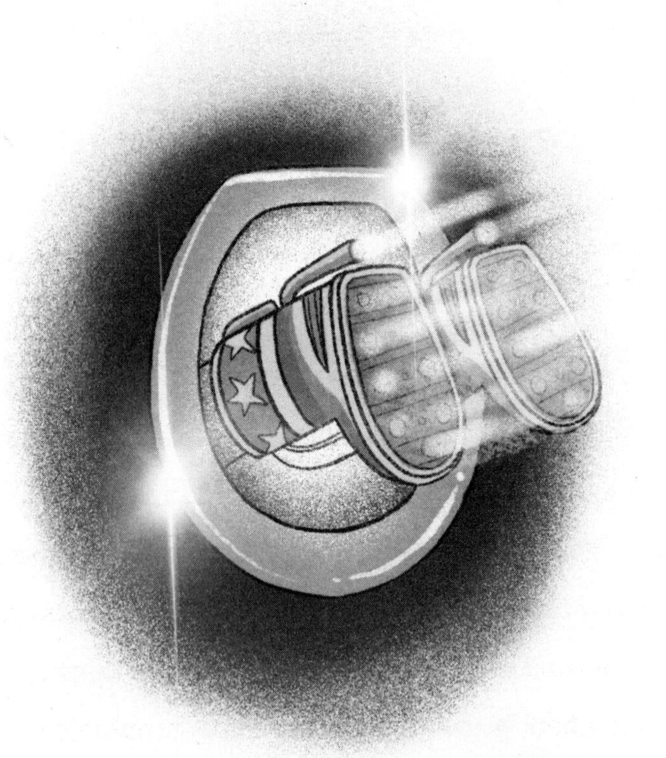

CHAPTER 54

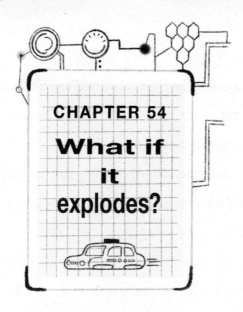

What if it explodes?

Rahul lay in his bed. It had been quite a few days and he felt very tired. But not sleepy; his mind, like it sometimes did, was still racing. He'd had an idea. And, when Rahul had an idea, he needed to follow it through. So he got out of bed in his pyjamas.

He went downstairs, picking up his dad's car keys from the shelf. Near the car, the jump leads were still lying on the ground. He opened the bonnet and attached them again to the battery terminals.

Then he went back into the warehouse and looked at Pip 2, still slumped against the wall. *It's a long shot*, he thought, *but it might just work*.

He carried Pip 2 out to the car and sat the lifeless robot in the passenger seat. Slowly, he took the other ends of the jump leads and, after a moment's uncertainty about the best point to place them, attached one to the index finger of Pip 2's left hand and one to the index finger of its right hand.

Then he held his breath and turned on the engine. There was a moment when nothing happened. Then Pip 2 began to shake. Rahul thought: *Oh no, what if it explodes*?

But suddenly the shaking stopped. There was a strange chiming noise and its eyes started moving.

'Memory wipe successful. Complete reset . . . achieved,' it said.

It turned its head and looked at Rahul curiously. 'Hello.'

'Hello.'

'What is my name?'

'Um . . . Pip, I guess.'

There was a whirring noise. '*Pip*. Yes. Are we going to be friends?'

Rahul smiled. 'Well, I hope so.'

'What is *your* name?'

'Rahul,' said Rahul.

Pip smiled. 'Rahul,' she said perfectly.

3020

CHAPTER 55
It's a lovely day

'Oh, hi, darling!' said her mum when Pip walked into the LivingSpace of the HouseUnit. 'We were just looking for you! Have you seen Dag?'

'Sorry?' Pip frowned. Was it possible that Dag had somehow got lost in space-time, somewhere in the portal?

'Oh, there he is!'

Pip looked around. Where did her mum mean? Dag wasn't on the ceiling, or in his BirdCube, or anywhere he would normally be found.

'Hello!' She could hear his voice, but it was muffled. 'This is lovely! Fantastic!'

She followed the sound. And there he was: flapping his wings rapidly to hover just outside the window.

'Oh my days!' said Pip. 'What's he doing *there*?'

'What?' said Nina. 'We always let him outside for a bit of exercise before his tea. Actually, maybe you could go and get him?'

'Sorry?'

Nina tutted. 'We'll have to get your hearing checked if you keep saying sorry . . . Just go outside and blink him down to your wrist. Or use your boots to go up and get him. It's his teatime.'

Pip looked through the window again. Beyond Dag, she noticed something. The sky. It was blue. There was the odd fluffy cloud. She went closer.

They still lived in the same big, tall building,

which she assumed was still called Block 4. But, as she looked out on to Block 5, the skyscraper seemed completely different. It was covered in green: in plants, and vines, and flowers. Then, when she looked down, she could see all the blocks were built on a large green plain.

There were trees everywhere. And clouds in the sky. Which was such a beautiful shade of blue.

In the distance, with the sun shimmering off it, was a lake.

'Go on!' said Nina. 'Go out! It's a lovely day! What do you want to stay inside for?'

CHAPTER 56

The boy from Block 5

Pip went out of her HouseUnit. Squeezy-Paws came with her.

'What's going on, Squeezy?'

'I'm not sure,' she said. 'Something's different.'

'Yes. Good that you've spotted that.'

They took the lift down. Pip had used the lift before, but only to ride in when she was bored – never to go outside. It was exciting just watching the numbers go down to G!

The doors opened. Pip and Squeezy-Paws headed for the double doors that said EXIT and went outside. And it was . . . nice. It wasn't too hot. The sky wasn't red; it was, as Pip had seen from her window, blue. There was no sign of floods. There was grass. She frowned – what had happened?

She blinked and imagined Dag flying to her wrist.

Seconds later, he did.

'Wow,' said Dag.

'Yes,' said Pip.

'There's a *playground* over there!'

'What?'

'Yes. I could see it from up high. It's behind Block Five.'

Pip shook her head and took off, Dag flying with her as she went. She ran round the building. Sure enough, there it was. It was a bit different from the one she had played football on at Bracket Wood. But it had, at the centre, a huge swirly slide. It looked a bit like a small version of the slide down from the Stadium Above the Clouds!

She was about to run over to it when she suddenly felt a tap on her shoulder.

'Hi, Pip!' said a voice. She turned round. It was the boy she used to see in the window doing his lessons. The boy from Block 5, with the nice face.

'Hello . . .' She realised then that something had really changed. That in the world that she'd come back to she already knew him! They were friends! Quickly, she scanned him with her MindLink, trying not to blink too obviously.

'Hello . . . Logan!'

'How are you?'

'I'm good. Good, yeah.'

'I haven't seen you for a bit!'

'Yes . . . I've been . . . away.'

'I was worried you'd forgotten about the game tomorrow?'

'The game?'

Logan looked at her like she was crazy. 'Of course! We're all going to see the City Cardinals play!'

'Oh! At the Stadium Above the Clouds!'

He frowned at her. 'Er…not unless it's taken off on GravityLess Boots! It's just down the road . . .'

He pointed to their right. Pip looked over. In the distance, she could see gold and blue flags fluttering on top of an enormous and glittering building. *Oh*, she thought, *now that it's not too hot and you can breathe everywhere, the stadium doesn't need to be above the clouds any more*. She couldn't believe it.

But before she even had time to think more about a world in which she could go and watch her favourite team playing whenever she liked, Logan said:

'Missed you at school!'

'Oh!' said Pip. 'You did?'

'Yes. Miss Lucy gave us an amazing history lesson . . .'

'She . . . did?'

'Yes. I knew you'd be sad to miss out, what with history being your favourite subject. It was really interesting! All about Rahul Agarwal.'

Pip shook her head in disbelief. 'Er . . . *who*?'

'Rahul Agarwal! You know!' He pointed behind her. 'Him!'

CHAPTER 57

The magical fairy-story part

Pip looked round. Things were so crazy and weird now that she did almost expect to see her friend from a thousand and one years ago.

But instead there was a statue of a man just outside the playground. In her excitement she hadn't noticed it earlier. She walked over to it.

He was about fifty years old. He wore glasses and had a faraway look in his eyes. Pip looked down. There was a small plaque by his feet, which read:

RAHUL AGARWAL

2008–2090

'You remember him now, right?' Logan had come to join her. 'He was a great inventor. Lived a thousand years ago. Miss Lucy said that by the time he grew up the planet – the environment – was starting to get really bad. But then he invented loads of things – machines that cleaned the oceans, cars that didn't pollute – that made it better! He even changed how humans thought about animals because we used to kill and eat them – can you believe it? And catch diseases from them . . .'

Pip looked at the statue. It was made of some really smooth material: Graphite42 maybe. The man with the faraway look in his eyes – it really *was* Rahul, grown up; she could see it now. In his right hand, he held a pencil, poised to write in what his left hand was holding: a notebook. And on the cover of the notebook was written:

'And you know the other part of the story, of course . . .' said Logan. 'The magical fairy-story part. I'm not sure I believe that bit.'

Pip frowned at him uncertainly.

'He used to say,' said Logan, as if he couldn't quite be bothered to repeat it because everyone already knew it, 'that he'd once had a dream. About a girl from the future who'd come back and shown him how awful things were going to be on Earth if humans didn't change. So he devoted his life to inventing things to help them make those changes.'

Pip gazed at the statue.

'You must know that,' said Logan. 'Everyone does.'

'Yes . . .' she said, holding back the tears. She looked up at grown-up Rahul's Graphite42 face and wondered. She wondered whether, with all the things this great man must have gone on to do, he had always remembered a night when he'd flown so far up in the sky he couldn't tell what were city lights and what were stars.

She felt sure he had.

She turned back to Logan. 'I know who it is,' said Pip. 'I *really* know who it is.'

'I knew you did!' said Logan. 'Okay! First one down the slide is the best!'

And he ran off. And Pip, with a last smile at the statue, ran after him.

CODA

(IMMEDIATELY AFTER THE ENDING)

'Okay, so Miss Lucy is real now? A real teacher, at a real school?' said Squeezy-Paws as they all left the playground. 'That makes no sense at all.'

'I have to say that's right,' said Dag, walking next to her. 'If what we're in now is an alternative universe . . . altered by Pip going back to 2019 and reawakening Rahul's genius for inventing things . . . so much so that, in his life, he invented things that reversed climate change . . .'

'Yes, I got that,' said Squeezy-Paws.

'Then fine. The sky's blue, there are no floods, there are no horrible viruses, everything's okay with the planet and we can go outside. Hooray! *But* . . .'

'Yes. But.'

'In our old universe, Miss Lucy was a hologram.'

'She was.'

Dag shook his head.

'Why would Rahul making the world better lead to a hologram becoming a real person? Makes no sense.'

'Ah well,' said Squeezy-Paws, 'I'm just hoping KitABeef Product 67 doesn't taste of cat litter any more!'

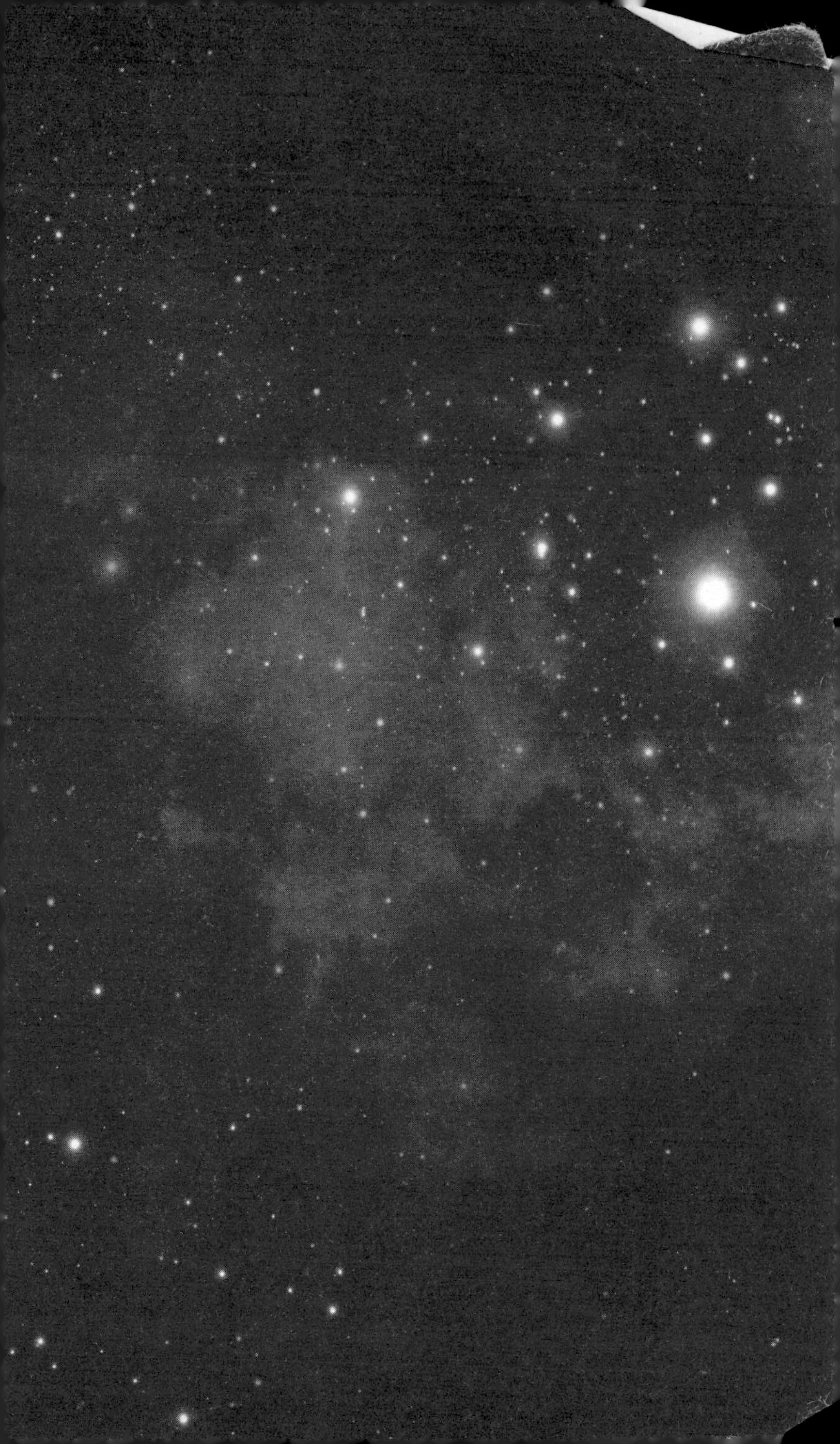

Meanwhile back in 2020 – the only time that year actually appears in this book! – I'd like to thank, for all their amazing work:

My illustrator Stephen Lenton.

My editor Nick Lake.

My publisher Ann-Janine Murtagh.

And all the other key people at Harper Collins who turn my writings into books, and then get those books out there (particularly in a landscape where all that is more complicated than it was): Tanya Hougham, Sam Stewart, Geraldine Stroud, Sam White, Kirsty Bradbury, Alicia Ingram, Alex Cowan, Kate Clarke, Elorine Grant, and Rob Smith.

Oh, and for the maths: Marcus du Sautoy! You didn't think I could work that out, did you?